"If you'll s[pend the night] with me, I'll let you off the hook..."

"I b-beg your pardon?" Star stammered dizzily.

He gazed back at her steadily, not a muscle moving in his lean, strong face. "One night. Tonight. That's the price."

She felt as if the ground had suddenly fallen away beneath her feet. "You're not serious...you can't be!"

"Why shouldn't I be serious?" Luc angled his well-shaped dark head back, a hard smile slanting his wide sensual mouth. "One night only.... After that, we never see each other again in this lifetime."

Her stomach twisted at that clarified picture. "But you don't want me—"

"Don't I?" Luc moved a fluid step closer. "Just one more time—"

"You don't want me. You never did! I'm not your type," Star argued as if she was repeating a personal mantra, a fevered, disbelieving edge to her voice.

"Except in bed," Luc added without hesitation.

LYNNE GRAHAM

One Night with His Wife

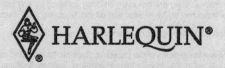

TORONTO • NEW YORK • LONDON
AMSTERDAM • PARIS • SYDNEY • HAMBURG
STOCKHOLM • ATHENS • TOKYO • MILAN • MADRID
PRAGUE • WARSAW • BUDAPEST • AUCKLAND

ISBN 0-373-12073-7

ONE NIGHT WITH HIS WIFE

First North American Publication 2000.

Visit us at www.romance.net

Printed in U.S.A.

CHAPTER ONE

'THE account no longer exists...' Star repeated that shattering announcement shakily under her breath as she walked back out of the bank.

In her hand, she still gripped the cheque she had tried unsuccessfully to cash. Beneath her shining fall of copper hair, her delicate features were stamped with shock, her aquamarine eyes bemused. She climbed back into Rory Martin's elderly classic car.

'Why were you so long?' Rory asked as he drove off.

Twisting round in her seat to check that the twins were still fast asleep in their car seats, Star muttered, 'I had to see the assistant manager—'

'That'll be because you're a lady of substance now,' Rory teased, referring to the money which Star had proudly paid into the bank only a few weeks earlier.

'And he told me that the account no longer exists,' Star confided abruptly.

At the traffic lights, Rory's fair hair swivelled. 'What are you talking about?'

'Juno has closed the account—'

'Your mother's done what?' Rory interrupted incredulously.

'There must be something badly wrong, Rory.'

'You're telling me. How could your mother close your account?' he demanded.

'It was *her* account.'

At that revelation, Rory sent Star a bewildered glance. 'Why didn't you have a bank account in your own name?'

'Because until last month when I sold those canvases, I

5

wouldn't have had anything to *put* in an account of my own,' Star stressed defensively. 'Juno was keeping me!'

Looking unimpressed by that argument, Rory pulled away from the traffic lights again. 'It was still *your* money in that account, the proceeds of the first couple of pictures you sold—'

His persistence made Star bristle with annoyance. 'Juno and I work on a "what's mine is yours" basis, Rory. We're family. We stick together. If she drew out that money, she must've needed it.' Then a further cause for alarm assailed her. 'Do you realise that it's over two weeks since I even *spoke* to my mother? Every time I call, all I get is that wretched answering machine!'

'I wouldn't be surprised if she's simply moved the account elsewhere and just forgotten to tell you about it,' Rory suggested in a soothing tone. 'Let's stop worrying about it. This *is* my day off. Where do you want to go next?'

Still in a bemused state, Star slowly shook her head. 'I can't go shopping without money—'

'So, I'll give you a loan to tide you over,' Rory slotted in with an easy shrug.

'No, thanks,' Star told him hurriedly, determined not to lean on him that way. 'You'd better just take us home again. I need to phone around and try to get hold of Juno to find out what's happening.'

'Be sensible, Star. She's hardly ever at home. Meanwhile, you *still* have to eat,' Rory pointed out with all the practicality of a male whose considerable family fortune was built on that same fact of life.

However, Star was immovable. Half an hour later, Rory drew up in the cobbled courtyard of a dilapidated fortified house complete with a tower surrounded by rusting scaffolding. Star lived rent-free as caretaker at Highburn Castle. The owner lived abroad. A friend of Juno's, he didn't have the money to maintain his inheritance, or the interest to apply for the grants available to repair a building listed as being of historical significance.

Star detached the belts from the baby seats in the back of the car. Rory unlocked the sturdy rear door of the castle and transported the first twin inside. Venus sighed in her sleep but remained comatose. Mars loosed an anxious little snort and shifted position. Both Star and Rory stilled until her restive son settled again. Mars had yet to prove the perceived wisdom that a baby could sleep through anything.

'They're great kids.' As they entered the big basement kitchen, Rory scrutinised the sleeping babies with the interest of a male who, as an only child, had had little contact with young children. 'I can never get over how tiny they are. When you think how premature they were, they're a right little pair of miracles!'

Having noticed the winking light on the answering machine which her mother had installed, Star gave him an abstracted nod. She switched on the tape and a familiar voice broke into speech.

'Star, it's me...I've got into some real hot water,' Juno gasped breathlessly into the sudden silence greeting her message. 'I haven't got time to explain, but I have to go abroad in a hurry and I had to borrow your money to pay for the flights! I'm absolutely skint. If I've left you in a hole, I'm sorry, but maybe you could contact Luc and get him to pay his dues for you and the twins...*please*, darling—'

'Who's Luc?' Rory demanded abruptly.

Star wasn't looking at him. She had jerked violently at the sound of that name. Her stomach somersaulting, she turned a whiter shade of pale. With an unsteady hand, she stopped the tape to absorb what she had so far heard and forcibly repressed all thought of Luc Sarrazin... Luc, her estranged husband, and the unwitting father of the twins.

What on earth had happened to the art gallery Juno was about to open in London? Only six weeks ago, Juno had been so confident of success. For goodness' sake, she had borrowed a small fortune to open that gallery! At the time, Star had been secretly astonished that *any* bank would give her mother such a large loan. Investing in Juno was a risky venture. Twice before, her mother had set up businesses which had failed.

And now it seemed that once again everything had fallen through. Star sighed. Where Juno was concerned that was nothing new. There was nothing new in her sudden dramatic flight from trouble either. That was vintage Juno, Star reflected sadly. When things went wrong, Juno panicked.

But now she urged her daughter to approach Luc Sarrazin for child support, Star simply cringed. Her mother might be desperate to justify her bahaviour, but that particular suggestion had been *way* below the belt. Juno knew what a disaster her daughter's short-lived marriage had been. Hadn't it been partly *her* fault that Luc had felt constrained to marry Star in the first place?

'Star…' Rory said again more forcefully.

'Shush! I need to hear the rest of this message.' Star switched the tape back on.

'I know you're trying to tune me out because I'm not saying what you want to hear. *Yes*, I hate Luc because he's a Sarrazin, but you made *babies* with him! He's got no heart or imagination but he ought to be keeping his own kids.' Juno paused. 'You see, I don't know how long it'll take to sort this mess out, or even if I'll be successful. But I promise you that *if* I am, I'm going to have the most wonderful surprise for you when I get back again!' she forecast in a bright but not very confident tone. 'Byee!'

'Luc…so his name's Luc,' Rory continued in a sharp, flat tone unfamiliar to Star's ears. 'I've never understood why you won't talk about the twins' father, but now that I've finally got his name, maybe you could tell me who he is.'

'My husband…well, sort of…' Star's voice just petered out again.

Rory's jaw had dropped. He pushed a dismayed hand through his fair hair, making it stand on end. 'You're saying you're married? But I thought—'

Star gave an awkward shrug. 'Yes, I know what you thought, but I couldn't see the point in contradicting you.'

'You saw no point?' His suntanned face was flushed, his hazel eyes bemused. 'There's a big difference between being a single mother and someone's *wife*, Star!'

'Is there? It wasn't a proper marriage and it only lasted a few weeks. The twins were an accident...*my* accident, *my* mistake,' Star stressed tautly. 'It wasn't something I wanted to talk about. It's something I just want to forget.'

'But you can't just *forget* you've got a husband!' Rory's dismay at that revelation was unconcealed. 'My parents will hit the roof if they find out that you're a married woman!'

It was make-your-mind-up time, Star conceded ruefully an hour later as she settled the twins into the wooden playpen with their toys. She had made a snack for their lunch from the few provisions that remained in the fridge. So where *was* she going with Rory?

Almost without her noticing, he had crossed the boundary of being just a good mate. But she could now pinpoint the exact date when that subtle change had begun. It had been the day he took her home to meet his family. Even though he had introduced her purely as the casual friend she had been at the time, his wealthy parents had seen her as a threat and acted accordingly. Rory had been embarrassed, and then furious at their behaviour. He was a decent guy, a really decent guy, and he had been a terrific friend.

They had met in the hospital canteen some weeks after the twins were born. The twins had been in the special care unit for a very long while. At the same time, Rory's beloved grandmother had been seriously ill. When he had realised that Star had to walk miles just to catch a bus to the hospital, he had started synchronising his visits to his grandmother's bedside and offering Star a lift home.

He'd been twenty-two then, and he had told her he worked in a supermarket. He hadn't mentioned that it was his year working out to complete a degree in business management, or the even more salient fact that his father *owned* a vast chain of supermarkets which was a household name in the UK.

When she had angrily accused him of not telling her the truth, he had said straight off, 'You've got a real prejudice against people with money.'

To be fair, she had not been very frank with Rory about her own past. She had told him that she had been a charity child, raised at a rich and reluctant French guardian's expense. The child had been kept rigorously at arm's length, lest she contaminate her guardian's good name and reputation with her unconventional background and questionable parentage.

Luc Sarrazin's father, Roland, had been that guardian.

And Star had only met Roland Sarrazin twice in her entire life. Once when she had first become his ward, at the age of nine, and the second and final time just over eighteen months earlier, when the old man had been dying. She had flown out to France to stay at the Sarrazins' magnificent family home, the Chateau Fontaine, and dutifully pay her respects. Her conscious mind now recoiled from remembering the other events which had taken place that winter.

Instead she recalled her years of separation from her mother, Juno Roussel. Nine years of prim and proper imprisonment in a boarding school for a child who had once known what it was to run free. Nine years deprived of even written contact with her mother. She had spent the school holidays in London, as the guest of Emilie Auber, an elderly childless widow related to the Sarrazin family. Only Emilie had given Star affection during those years, but Emilie had also made the appalling mistake of encouraging Star to love Luc Sarrazin.

Dear sweet Emilie, with her sentimental dreams of romance...

'Luc needs someone like you, but he doesn't know it yet,' Emilie had said.

No, Luc definitely *hadn't* known. And he hadn't needed her either. Indeed, Luc had given Star a taste of humiliation which she would never, ever forget.

'You're not in love with me. You're in love with sex. Find a boy the same age and experiment on him!'

As Star stared into space, she shivered and hugged herself. The chill inside her seemed to bite right through to her bones. It had been eighteen months, and she hadn't yet followed Luc's advice and experimented. First she had discovered that that single reckless night in Luc's bed had got her pregnant. Then she had become the mother of two tiny premature babies. The twins' tenuous hold on life had sentenced her to months of tortured fear and anxiety. But now Venus and Mars were home, safe and healthy, and slowly catching up with their peers. And Rory was *still* here, being caring and supportive. He loved the twins and he wanted a girlfriend, not just a mate. He wasn't likely to wait for her to make up her mind for ever…

His kisses were pleasant. They didn't burn. But then being burned *hurt*, Star reminded herself fiercely. No more dancing too close to the fire. No more dizzy adolescent fantasising. The guy she loved, the only guy she had ever loved, had spent their wedding night in the arms of his exquisitely beautiful mistress, Gabrielle Joly. As rejections went, it had been pretty final. It had told her all she should have needed to know. But Star had always been a fighter, and stubborn with it. She hadn't been willing to let go of her dream. Hating Luc, loving Luc, and determined to hang onto him by any means available, she had got down and dirty in the trenches of fighting for her man.

Getting him into bed had felt like a major coup. She had thought she had won; she had thought he was *hers*; she had thought surrender meant acceptance. She hadn't really cared how *he* felt about it. After all, men didn't always know what was good for them. In fact men could be pretty thick about recognising their soulmate if she came along in an unfamiliar guise. And Luc, even possessed as he was of an IQ of reputedly sky-high proportions, had been a really slow and exceedingly stubborn learner.

'Look—'

Star glanced up.

Rory was watching her with a rueful smile. 'I've got some things to do. I might call back later this evening.'

For a split second, Star studied him with blank eyes. Then she coloured and finally pulled free of her troubled thoughts. 'OK...sorry, I was miles away.'

As she saw Rory out, she was conscious of a guilty sense of relief. Thinking about Luc had shaken her up and filled her with angry frustration. But regretting her mistakes was currently an unproductive waste of time. She would be far better occupied worrying about how she was to feed herself and the twins when Juno had left her literally penniless!

It was going to be a wild night, Luc Sarrazin acknowledged. On the exposed hill road, the wind buffeted his powerful car, forcing him to keep a hard grip on the steering wheel. But the gale-force wind was a mere breeze in comparison to the cold and lethal anger Luc was containing behind his habitually cool façade.

The day before, Emilie Auber's accountant had flown to Paris to request an urgent meeting with Luc. Robin Hodgson had been the anxious bearer of bad news. Without consulting her accountant, or indeed anybody else, Emilie had loaned practically every penny she possessed to a woman called Juno Roussel.

Luc had been furious. But he had also been grimly amused that even in such trying circumstances Emilie had not admitted the embarrassing reality that Juno Roussel was in fact *his* mother-in law! The mother-in-law from hell, Luc conceded with a curled lip. He hadn't been remotely surprised to learn that Juno had since disappeared without repaying the trusting Emilie any of the money she had borrowed.

'I believe that from the outset of this unpleasant business there was a deliberate intent to defraud your father's cousin,' Hodgson had then gone on to contend heavily. 'Emilie was first introduced to Juno Roussel by a young woman she had known as a child—the Roussel woman's daughter, Star.'

That information had genuinely shaken Luc. The suggestion that Star might have been involved in ripping off Emilie had turned his stomach; Star had always been so honest.

However, what had truly shattered his legendary nerves of steel during that interview was hearing the entirely incidental news that Star had apparently become the mother of twins. Infants still in hospital at the time of Star's visit to Emilie last autumn. A *mother*...Luc's teenage bride, Luc's runaway wife. Star had given birth to another man's children while she was still *his* wife!

Luc had been incandescent at that revelation. He recalled little beyond that point. And he *still* felt wild with rage. He wanted to smash something; he wanted blood to flow. How dared Star do something so sordid? How dared she run around sleeping with other men while she was still legally married to him? But then she was faithfully following in her mother's footsteps, wasn't she? Juno, whose dangerous influence he had impulsively tried to protect her from. What a fool he had been to have any faith in the daughter of a blackmailer!

No doubt Star currently believed herself safe from retribution. In spite of all his efforts over the past eighteen months, Luc had been unable to find out where his runaway wife was living. But that very morning Luc had obtained entrance to the art gallery which Juno had abandoned. There he had found the address book which the older woman had left behind in her hasty departure...

That evening, Star had just finished settling the twins into their cots when the ancient front doorbell shrilled noisily on the old servants' call board in the kitchen. Only a stranger would go to the front entrance, which was hardly ever used. Indeed, the bolts had long since rusted into place. But, even though there was a sign directing all callers to the rear entrance, it was amazing how many people chose to ignore it.

Not in the mood to rush out of the back door and trudge all the way round to the front, Star groaned. The bell shrieked again in two long, ferocious bursts. She tensed, wondering if urgent need lay behind such unreasonable impatience. Perhaps a walker had been injured or a car had crashed out on the road.

She raced out into the teeth of the wind that had been rising steadily throughout the day. It blasted her copper hair back from her brow and plastered her long fringed skirt to her legs, making it difficult for her to move quickly. As she struggled round the wall into shelter, she winced at the racket the scaffolding was making as it rattled in the gale.

The first thing her attention centred on was a stunningly expensive sports car, with a sleek golden bonnet. With disconcertion, her gaze whipped from the car to the tall, dark male positioned by the Victorian bellpull. Luc...it was Luc! But how *could* it be Luc? With Emilie Auber sworn to secrecy about her whereabouts, how could he possibly have found out where she was living?

The sheer shock of recognition stopped Star dead in her tracks. A wave of disorientating dizziness currented through her. She rocked back unsteadily on her heels and shivered violently in reaction. Registering her presence, Luc strode towards her, his devastatingly dark and handsome face hard as granite.

Huge aquamarine eyes fixed to him as her head tipped back to take in all of him. He was so big. Somehow she had forgotten *how* big. There he stood, six feet three inches of potent masculine intimidation, exuding a twenty-two-carat sophistication that came as naturally to him as breathing. He was, after all, one of the most powerful investment bankers in the world. He had the sleek, honed elegance of a prowling jaguar and a physical presence that was sheer intimidation.

Eyes dark as midnight glittered down like shards of ice crystal into Star's. A pulse at the base of her slender throat beat convulsively fast and made it impossible for her to catch her breath.

'Shock...horror,' Luc enumerated with a sibilant softness that trickled down her sensitive spine like a hurricane warning. 'You still wear every thought and feeling on your face, *mon ange*.'

While *he* still showed nothing, Star reflected in feverish abstraction, her attention glued to the smooth, hard planes of his lean, strong face. 'Luc...' she managed in a choky little voice before the tidal wave of horribly familiar guilt engulfed her and reduced her to squirming silence instead.

'*Oui*, your husband,' Luc drawled, his husky French accent dramatising every syllable with the most incredibly sexy edge.

A tide of colour washed over Star's triangular face. She shut her eyes in dismay at that last forbidden thought about his accent and struggled to get a grip on herself.

'Surely you expected me to track you down sooner or later?'

'Not really, no...' Star mumbled, eyes shooting wide again to telegraph a look of naked panic. She was trying to picture herself telling him the most unwelcome news he would probably ever hear. That he was the father of twelve-month-old twins.

Luc's beautifully modelled wide, sensual mouth compressed into a hard line. 'Guilt is written all over you!' he ground out in icy disgust.

He *knew*. He knew about the twins! What else could he be talking about? He must have leant on poor Emilie and browbeaten her into spilling the beans. And he wasn't wrong about the guilt. At that moment, Star was just eaten alive by that sensation, and at the same time savagely hurt. It had been one thing to imagine how Luc might react, quite another to be confronted with the brutal reality of that rejection.

CHAPTER TWO

'*ALORS!*' Luc slung the noisy scaffolding girding the castle frontage a grim appraisal. 'Take me inside,' he instructed in imperious command.

'The front door doesn't open...you'll have to come round the back.' Alarmingly conscious of Luc powering along beside her, impatiently curtailing his long stride to her smaller steps, Star hurried breathlessly back round to the rear of the castle.

'I'm so s-sorry, Luc...I really am,' she stammered truthfully in the dim passageway which led past several doors into the basement kitchen. It was her only reception area, and although daylight was only just beginning to fade she already had candles lit, because it was a dark room, and the place needed rewiring.

One step into the kitchen, Luc surveyed her with dark eyes colder than frostbite. 'By the time I have finished taking this betrayal out of your useless little hide, you'll understand the *true* meaning of what it feels like to be sorry!'

Shaken by such a level of condemnation, Star turned even paler. Did he think that she should have terminated her pregnancy? Was that what he was getting at? Had it been a betrayal of trust to give birth to children he would not have wanted her to have? Her tummy muscles knotted up. 'Sometimes things just g-go wrong, Luc—'

'Not in my life they don't...not once until *you* came along,' he completed with icy exactitude.

In the face of an accusation that she was aware had more than a smidgen of truth, Star braced herself with one nerveless hand on the back of the sagging armchair by the range and stared helplessly at him, registering every detail of his appearance. His superb charcoal-grey silk suit sheathed his broad shoulders and the long, powerful length of leg in the kind of fabulous fit only obtainable from extremely expensive tailoring. His luxuriant black hair had been ruffled by the wind, but the excellence of the cut had ensured that the springy dark gleaming strands just fell back into place.

Briefly engaged in sparing his humble domestic surroundings a grim, lip-curling appraisal, Luc turned his attention back to her without warning.

Flash! As Star collided with the long-lashed brilliance of his stunning dark deep-set eyes, it was like finding herself thrust into an electric storm. Heat speared through her slight frame. Feverish pink sprang up over her slanted cheekbones. She trembled, every sense awakened to painful life and sensitivity, an intense awareness of her own body engulfing her to blur every rational thought.

Silence banged thunderously in her ears, her heart thumping a frantic tattoo against her breastbone. A wanting so powerful it left her weak had seized her, dewing her skin with perspiration, stealing her ability to breathe or vocalise. What was it about him? She had asked herself that so many times. The obvious? He *was* fantastically good-looking. So tall, so dark and beautifully built. His maternal grandmother had been an Italian countess. That heritage was etched in his fabulous bone structure, the blue-black ebony of his hair and the golden hue of his skin.

Was that really the *only* reason she yearned for him with every fibre of her being and when deprived of him, felt only half alive? It had to be the only reason, she told herself frantically.

'So you have nothing to say for yourself,' Luc drawled.

'I'm still in shock,' she mumbled truthfully.

Shock. *Her* shock was nothing to *his*, Luc decided with sudden ferocity. To find her living like this in abject poverty, candles lighting a room Gothic in its lack of modern conveniences or comfort. She was dressed like a gipsy and thin as a rail. Bereft of the support of Sarrazin money for just eighteen months, she'd clearly sunk without trace. Just as he had expected; just as he had forecast. He studied her bare feet, recalled that she had almost run across the rough gravel, and the most extraordinary ache stirred inside him. Frustrated fury leapt up to engulf and crush it out. Not enough sense to come in out of the rain, Emilie had once said of Star.

Emilie... Luc's quick intellect zoomed in on that timely reminder at supersonic speed, but his hooded gaze was nonetheless still engaged on roaming up over Star's veiling skirt with its silky fringe. Memory unerringly supplied a vision of the slender, shapely perfection of her legs. He tensed almost imperceptibly, his appraisal rising higher, finding no escape in the pouting thrust of her small braless breasts beneath her velvet wrap top.

As she flung her head back, his lean, powerful body hardened in urgent all-male response. Her hair glowed in the dimness, bright as beaten copper in sunlight, dancing round her triangular face. Her pallor highlighted exotic eyes, alive with awakening sensuality, and a wide, soft, voluptuously pink mouth.

And *this* was the woman he had spent over a hundred thousand pounds trying to trace over the past eighteen months? Tiny, skinny, irredeemably different from the rest of her sex. There was nothing conventional in her mercurial changes of expression, her fluid restive movements, her jangling bracelets, her outrageous earrings shaped like cats or her ridiculous clothing. She wasn't beautiful either. There was nothing there that he admired or looked for in a woman—nothing but the drugging, earthy sexuality that was as much a part of her as her dusty bare feet, Luc told himself with driven determination.

Star had the soul and spirit of a small wild animal, always ready to fight for survival and use whatever she had to get what she wanted. Or *trade*? Why else was she surveying him with that melodramatically charged look of undeniable hun-

ger? No, there was no doubt in Luc's mind that Star knew
exactly what he was here about. To look so ashamed and
desperate, she had to have been involved up to her throat in
persuading his father's elderly cousin to part with her money!

'How could you have done such a thing to Emilie?' Luc
demanded icily.

A frown line indented Star's smooth brow. Colliding with
his glittering dark gaze, she froze as if an icy hand had
touched her heart. Perspiration beaded her short upper lip.
Gooseflesh sprang up on her exposed skin. The chill he em-
anated was that powerful.

'Emilie...?' Star's frown line deepened.

'The loan, Star.'

'What loan...what are you talking about?'

'*Si tu continues...*' Luc swore so softly that the tiny hairs
at the nape of Star's neck rose.

It was a threat. If she kept it up, he would get angry. But,
Emilie and what loan?

'I honestly don't know what—'

Luc slowly spread the long brown fingers of one expressive hand. The atmosphere was so charged she could almost
feel it hiss warningly in her pounding eardrums. 'So that's
the way you're trying to play it,' he spelt out, framing each
laden word with terrifying emphasis. 'You're acting all
ashamed because of the two little bastards you've managed
to spawn while you were still married to me?'

The offensive words struck Star in the face like a blow.
She fell back in physical retreat. 'Bastards?' she whispered
tremulously.

'Illegitimacy seems to run very much in your family genes,
doesn't it?' Luc pointed out lethally. 'Your children...
you...your mother—not one of you born with anything so
conventional as a church blessing.'

Registering in disbelief that Luc believed that their twin
babies had been fathered by some other man, Star gazed back

at him with haunted eyes of bewildered pain. 'No…*no*,
Luc…I—'

'Surely you don't think I require an explanation?' Luc elevated a winged ebony brow, studying her with sardonic dis-
dain. 'I shall divorce you for adultery and will *not* pay ali-
mony, I assure you.'

Divorce…*divorce*! Even in the midst of her appalled incredulity that Luc should believe her capable of giving birth
to another man's children while still legally joined to him,
that single word tore into Star like a bullet slamming into her
body. And like a bullet rending tender flesh it brought un-
imaginable pain. Divorce was for ever and final. She stared
back at him, eyes shadowing, slanted cheekbones taut with
tension beneath her fair skin.

A roughened laugh escaped Luc. 'You seem shocked.'

The atmosphere sizzled, hot with high-voltage tension. She
sensed his rage, battened down beneath the icy façade he
maintained. And aching, yearning sadness filled her to overflowing when she saw the grim satisfaction in his hard, dark
gaze. Now he had the perfect excuse to be rid of her. But
then he'd had excuse enough in any case. Not wanted, not
suitable. Too young, too lowly born, possessed of embarrassing relations, unfit to be the wife of the chairman of a
bank.

'You should never have married me…' Anguish filled Star
as she remembered her ridiculous optimism against all the
odds. Her manipulation, her manoeuvres, her final desperate
attempt to force him to give her a trial as a real wife. What
did it matter if he now chose to believe that the twins belonged to some other man? It had to be what he wanted to
believe. He didn't care; he had *never* cared.

Luc had swung away. His strong profile was rigid. He
clenched his hands into fists and then slowly uncurled them
again. But he could still feel the violence like a flickering
flame darting along the edge of his self-control. She was a
little slut. He despised her. In the circumstances, he was be-

ing wonderfully polite and civilised. Only he didn't feel civilised. He wanted to punish her. He wanted to punish her
even more when she stood there like a feckless child, who
never, ever thought of the damage she might be doing. But
he didn't dare risk acting on that urge.

For eighteen endless months he had had Star on his conscience. He had worried himself sick about her. How she was
living, *where* she was living, even whether or not she was
still living. In Luc's opinion, anyone with her capacity for
emotional intensity had to be unstable. She had too much
emotion, the most terrifying amount of emotion, and it had
all been focused solely on him.

Eighteen months ago, in more anger than he had ever
known, he had lashed out and ripped her apart with the force
of his rejection. And she had taken off like a bat out of hell,
leaving all her clothes behind, not to mention a letter which
Luc had considered dangerously close to thoughts of self-
destruction. He had had the moat dragged at the chateau, he
had had frogmen in the lake day after day...

Sarrazin Bride Driven to Suicide by Unfeeling Husband.
He had imagined the headlines. Over and over again, he had
dreamt of her floating like the Lady of Shalott or Ophelia
surrounded by lilies. He had been *haunted* by her! Freed of
her ludicrous expectations, he should have found peace.
Instead, he had got his nice quiet life back, and his freedom,
but he had lived in *hell*!

Star studied Luc with pitying aquamarine eyes and tilted
her chin. 'You weren't worthy of my love. You were never
worthy of my love. I can see that now.'

Luc swung back to face her as if she had plunged a dagger
into his strong back. Black eyes cold as charity assailed hers.

'You're unreachable. You're going to turn into a man as
miserable and joyless as your father,' Star forecast with a
helpless shake of her copper head. 'You don't even *like* children, do you?'

Luc stared back at her in silent derision, but the slight

darkening of colour over his spectacular cheekbones, his sudden tension and the flare of hostility burning from him told her all she needed to know. Oh, yes, some day a recognised son and heir would be born to his next wife, Star reflected painfully. And Luc would naturally repeat all the cruelties of his own lonely childhood. What else did he know? That child would be banished to a distant nursery and a strict nanny. He would be taught to behave like a miniature adult and censured for every childish reaction until he learned not to cry, not to shout, not to lose control...indeed that emotions were messy, unnecessary and unmanly. At least that poor stifled child would not be Mars, Star told herself wretchedly.

'Emilie...' Luc reminded Star with icy bite. 'How *could* you introduce Emilie to a vulture like your mother?'

Thrown into total confusion by that abrupt and confusing change of subject, Star had to struggle to recall the loan which Luc had mentioned earlier, but she could not stretch her mind to comprehend how anyone could possibly call Juno a vulture. Juno would give her last penny to anyone in need. 'I don't understand—'

'*Bon! Cela suffit maintenant...* OK, that's enough,' Luc incised harshly, his darkly handsome features cold and set. 'Lies are going to make me even angrier. In fact, lies may just prompt me to calling in the police!'

Lies? The police? *The police?* Star's lashes lowered to screen her shaken eyes as she fought to concentrate her wandering thoughts. How much more did Luc expect from her? All right, so he acknowledged few human feelings and therefore could not understand what she was going through right now. But he arrived here without warning, disgustingly referred to their children as having been 'spawned', simply assumed that they had been fathered by a lover and then he announced that he wanted a divorce! Wasn't that enough to be going on with?

'I don't tell lies,' she stated.

'That should make life simpler. So, you and Juno collaborated to persuade Emilie to loan your mother everything she had—'

'*No…*' Star stepped forward in aghast disconcertion at that charge.

'Yes. Don't you dare lie to me,' Luc intoned in a low, vicious tone she had never heard or thought to hear from him. 'Yesterday, Emilie's accountant told me the whole story. Emilie cashed in her investments and gave Juno the money to open up that art gallery.'

Star froze. The pieces of the puzzle finally fell into place. Juno had borrowed from Emilie, *not* from a bank!

'And now Juno's vanished. Are you going to tell me where she is?'

'I don't know where she is…' Horrified by what she was now finding out, Star spun away in an uncoordinated movement.

As she reconsidered the message which Juno had left on the answering machine, her temples tightened with tension. Now she knew why her parent had fled the country at such speed. And no wonder Juno hadn't explained the nature of the 'hot water' she was in! Her mother would have known just how shocked and disgusted her daughter would be at her behaviour.

Juno had lied by omission, deliberately concealing the fact that her loan had come from Emilie. Had Star had the smallest suspicion that Emilie was considering backing the art gallery venture, she would have stepped in and stopped it happening. But how could Emilie have been so naive? Emilie was neither rich nor foolish. So why on earth had she risked her own security to loan money to a woman she hardly knew?

'You're not prepared to rat on Juno, are you?' Luc condemned harshly.

'I'm not in a position to!' Star protested.

Luc studied her with hard, dark eyes. 'Emilie has been left without a sou.'

'Oh…*no!*' Distress and shame filled Star to overflowing. She loved Emilie Auber very much. That her own mother should have accepted Emilie's money and then run away sooner than deal with the fall-out when things went wrong truly appalled Star.

But she had one minor comfort. Luc would not allow Emilie to suffer. He would replace her lost funds without question or hesitation. His reputation for ruthless financial dealing would not get in the way of his soft spot for the kindly older woman. Juno would have known that too, Star reflected bitterly. Was that how her mother had justified herself when she had borrowed money which Emilie could ill afford to offer?

'If you tell me where Juno has gone, I might begin to believe that you have nothing to do with this disgraceful business,' Luc murmured very softly.

'I told you…I don't know!' Star flung him a shimmering glance of feverish anxiety. 'How could I have anything to do with this? How could you even *think* that I would have encouraged Emilie to loan money to my mother?'

'Why not?' Luc dealt her a grim appraisal. 'Aside of that one visit you made with your mother in the spring, Emilie has neither seen nor heard anything from you since you left France. That doesn't suggest any great affection on your side of the fence, does it, *mon ange*?'

Star braced slender hands on the scrubbed pine table and stiffened with instant resentment at that accusation. But she could not admit that she had maintained regular contact with Emilie without christening Emilie a liar for pretending otherwise to Luc.

'I can't believe that you think I could've been involved in this in any way,' Star reasserted with determined spirit.

'You're not that innocent. How could you be? You're Juno's daughter. And living like this…' Luc cast a speaking glance round the bare kitchen. 'It must've been very tempting to think up a way of hitting back at me.'

'I don't think like that—'

'Your mother does. She hates my family. Emilie may only be a cousin of my late father's, but she is still a member of my family.'

'Luc…I wouldn't let anyone harm Emilie in any way!' Star argued frantically.

'So why did you introduce her to Juno?'

'Why wouldn't I have? Emilie had always wanted to meet her. I could never have dreamt Juno would ask her for a loan, or that Emilie would even *consider* giving her money!'

Star raised unsteady hands and pressed them against her taut face in a gesture of frustration. Why would Emilie have loaned money to Juno when she *knew* that Juno was hopeless with money? It didn't make sense.

'Do you want to know why Emilie gave your mother that money?'

Star nodded slowly.

'Emilie thought that if the gallery got off the ground, you would move up to London and live with Juno. Emilie was hoping to see more of *you.*'

Every scrap of remaining colour drained from beneath Star's skin. She twisted away on driven feet, her face stricken. She wanted to cover her ears from Luc's derisive tone of condemnation. She also wanted to get her hands on her irresponsible, flighty parent and shake her until her teeth rattled in her pretty blonde head.

'I hold you responsible for all of this,' Luc delivered in cold completion.

Star's slight shoulders bowed. 'I honestly didn't know about the loan—'

'I don't believe you. When you first saw me this evening, your guilty conscience betrayed you.' Luc strolled fluidly towards the door. 'Since I'm not getting any satisfaction here, I'll go to the police.'

Star whirled round, aquamarine eyes aghast. 'Luc… no…*please* don't do that!'

Luc shrugged a broad shoulder. '"Please" doesn't work with me any more. I want blood. I want Juno. If you can't deliver her, I'm just wasting my time, and I don't like people who waste my time.'

'If I knew where she was, I'd tell you...I *swear* I would!' Star gasped, hurrying across the expanse of worn slate floor that separated them.

'No, you wouldn't. You'd protect her. You'd hide her from me—'

'No... If she got in touch...' Star snatched in a shuddering breath, her eyes overbright with unshed tears. 'I'd tell you. I swear I would. I wouldn't like doing it, but what Juno's done to Emilie hurts and angers me very much. My mother was in the wrong—'

'The police can deal with her. I've got enough to hang her with.'

'No...you can't do that!' Involuntarily, she stretched out her hand and pulled at his arm in an attempt to hold him back as he opened the door that led into the passageway.

Luc gazed down at her, eyes glittering black and cold as ice in warning. 'Don't touch me...'

Her throat closed over. Her fingers dropped jerkily from his sleeve. She trembled in shock, a mortified wave of hot colour sweeping up her throat. For an instant, she sank like a stone into a bottomless pit of remembered rejection. Their wedding night, which Luc had spent with his beautiful mistress. The unbelievable anguish of loving without return. In a split second she relived it all, aquamarine eyes darkening with pain and veiling.

'I'll crucify Juno in court and I'll divorce you,' Luc murmured with velvet-soft sibilance.

'Do you want me to get down on my knees and *beg*?' Star flung at him wildly.

Luc raised a withering aristocratic dark brow.

'I'll do *anything*—'

'Begging doesn't excite me.'

Startled by that husky assurance, Star lifted her head and looked up at him again. Luc gave her a dark smile, brilliant eyes shimmering beneath his lush black lashes. Heat curled low in the pit of her stomach, jolting her. She quivered, drawn like a moth to a flame.

'But then I like my women tall and blonde and rather more sophisticated,' Luc completed with dulcet cool.

Star flinched, stomach turning over at that lethal retaliation.

In the simmering silence the door at the foot of the dim passageway was suddenly thrust noisily wide. Rory strode in, carrying several bulging supermarket carrier bags. He came to a halt with a startled frown. 'Sorry. When you didn't hear me knock, I tried the door. I didn't realise you had company.'

Disconcerted by Rory's appearance, Star breathed in deep. 'Rory, this is Luc…Luc Sarrazin. He's just leaving—'

'Like hell I will,' Luc incised, half under his breath, still as a statue now by her side.

Not believing her ears at that intervention, Star glanced at her estranged husband in astonishment.

'Luc…?' The bags of groceries in Rory's hands slid down onto the stone floor as he released his grip on them. 'You're…you're Star's *husband*?'

Luc ignored him. His attention was on Star. 'Does he live here?'

'No, I don't,' Rory stated curtly.

Luc turned his arrogant head back to study Rory. *'Fiches le camp*…get out of here!'

'I'm not leaving unless Star asks me to…' The younger man stood his ground.

'If you stay, I'll rearrange your face,' Luc asserted with cool, unapologetic provocation.

'Stop it, Luc!' Star was aghast at Luc's unashamed aggression.

Luc angled back his proud dark head and lounged back

against the doorframe like a big powerful jungle cat ready to spring. 'Stop what?'

'What's got into you?' Star demanded in hot embarrassment.

'This little punk got my wife pregnant and you dare to ask me that?' Luc launched back at her, his husky accent scissoring over every syllable with raw incredulity.

'Rory is *not* the father of my children!' Star slammed back at him shakily.

Rory shot a thoroughly bemused look at both of them.

Luc had stilled again. His nostrils flared. His breath escaped in an audible hiss of reaction at that news. 'So how many experiments did it take?' he derided in disgust.

Star was ashen pale. She said nothing. Turning away, she closed a taut hand over Rory's arm and walked him back outside. 'I'm sorry about this, but it's better if you go for now. Luc and I need to talk, sort some things,' she explained tightly.

'Obviously you haven't told him about the twins yet.'

'No…but he wants a divorce,' she heard herself advance, because she was too ashamed to tell Rory what her mother had done to Emilie.

Rory sighed. 'Probably the best thing in the circumstances. He seems a pretty aggressive character. I couldn't see you ever being happy with someone like that.'

Happy? She almost laughed. What was happy? Being separated in every way from Luc had been like living in a void. It hadn't cured her. Forcing a brittle smile, Star said, 'Tomorrow, I'm going to have a row with you about buying food for us.'

Closing the back door again, she leant against the solid wood, mustering all her strength. She had assumed that Luc had gone back into the kitchen. So as she moved back in that direction she was surprised to see that the twins' bedroom door had been pressed more fully open.

Luc was poised several feet from the foot of the cots.

Venus was curled on her side, an adorable thatch of copper curls screening her tiny face. Mars was flat on his back, silky dark hair fringing his sleep-flushed features, one anxious hand gripping the little bunny rattle which he never liked to get too far from him.

'They're what? Five...six months old?' Luc queried without an ounce of emotion.

After the number of setbacks the twins had weathered, they were still quite small for their age. Star studied her children with her heart in her eyes, thanking God as she did every time she came into this room that they had both finally been able to come home to her, whole and healthy. She glanced from under her lashes at Luc. His bold dark profile was grim.

'Would you have liked them to be yours?' she heard herself whisper foolishly.

'Tu plaisantes!'

You must be joking! Star reddened fiercely at that retort. What a stupid question to ask! Instead of asking it, she should just have told him the truth. Whether Luc liked it or not, Venus and Mars, fancifully christened by Juno, *were* his son and daughter.

Luc strode out past her. Leaving the door carefully ajar, Star followed him back into the kitchen.

'In fact, I'm extremely grateful that they are *not* my children,' Luc drawled in level continuation as he took up a commanding stance by the hearth, his lean, dark, devastating features cool as ice. 'It would have complicated the divorce and made a clean break impossible. Considering that we have about as much in common as oil and water, joint custody would have been a serious challenge.'

Star was pale as death now. His reaction shook her to her very depths. All right, so he had never thought of her as his wife. Yet when Rory had walked in Luc had been angry, aggressive, powered, it had seemed, by some atavistic all-male territorial instinct. She had never seen that side of him before, but now she had to accept that his reaction to Rory had simply stemmed from his savage pride.

Didn't he have any normal feelings at all? How could Luc just stand there telling her that he was relieved and grateful that her babies were supposedly nothing to do with him? In pained fascination, she searched his face, absently noting the very faint sheen of moisture on his dark golden skin, the unyielding blank darkness of his hooded gaze.

'Luc...I—'

'I was leaving...' Luc studied his diminutive wife, struggling to distance himself, black fury like a thick, suffocating smoke fogging his usually ordered thoughts. Suddenly he understood why so many unfaithful wives had ended up losing their heads to Madame Guillotine during the French Revolution. Feeling the slight tremor in his hands, he dug them rawly into the pockets of his well-cut pants. *Nobody will ever love you as much as I do.* Such soft words, such empty promises. He was *not* a violent man. But he wanted to remind her who she belonged to. No, she did *not* belong to him, he adjusted at grim speed. He did not *want* her to belong to him. He had meant every word he had said.

Star moved anxious hands. 'Could we just talk?'

'Talk?' Luc growled, not quite levelly, watching the way the flickering candlelight played over her porcelain-fine skin, accentuating the distinctive colour of her eyes and the full, inviting softness of her ripe mouth.

'About Juno?' Star moistened her dry lips with the tip of her tongue and watched Luc tense, his stunning dark eyes welding to her with sudden force.

'No.'

'No?' Colour mantled Star's cheekbones as the raw tension in the atmosphere increased. Her heart skipped a beat and then began to thump against her ribcage. Her mouth running dry, she tensed in dismay as she felt her breasts lift and swell, the rosy peaks tightening into mortifying prominence.

Luc's brilliant eyes flamed over her. 'If you spend the night with me, I'll let you both off the hook…'

'I b-beg your pardon?' Star stammered dizzily.

'I won't put the police on Juno's trail.' He gazed back at her steadily, not a muscle moving in his lean, strong face. 'One night. Tonight. That's the price.'

Her soft full mouth fell open. She closed it again, and tried and failed to swallow. She felt as if the ground had suddenly fallen away beneath her feet. 'You're not serious…you can't be!'

The silence shimmered like a heatwave between them.

Star trembled.

'Why shouldn't I be serious?' Luc angled his well-shaped dark head back, a hard smile slanting his wide, sensual mouth. 'One night only. Then tomorrow you travel down to London with me to see Emilie. Together we reassure her that she has nothing further to worry about. After that, we never see each other again in this lifetime.'

Her stomach twisted at that clarified picture. 'But you don't want me—'

'Don't I?' Luc moved a slow, fluid step closer, dark eyes mesmerically intense as they scanned her bemused face. 'Just one more time…'

'You don't want me. You never did! I'm not your type,' Star argued, as if she was repeating a personal mantra, a fevered, disbelieving edge to her voice.

'Except in bed,' Luc extended without hesitation.

Star stilled in astonishment. Then she jerked in reaction to that revelation. He was finally acknowledging a fact he had refused to concede eighteen months earlier. Luc *could* find her desirable. The night the twins had been conceived, Luc had genuinely responded to *her*, not just to the anonymous invitation of a female body in his bed. The following morning, his cold silence on that point had shattered what little had remained of her pride.

Anger and regret now foamed up inside her in a bewildering surge. 'Couldn't you just have admitted that to me eighteen months ago?'

'No,' Luc drawled smoothly. 'It would have encouraged you to believe that our marriage had a future.'

The heat still singing through Star's blood suddenly slowed and chilled. Such cool calculation stabbed her to the heart and unnerved her.

'But that was then and this is *now*,' Luc stressed with syllabic sibilance.

Now, she repeated to herself in reminder. Now, when Luc had knocked her sideways by suggesting that they spend one last night together. Why not? With his customary cool he had already boxed her in with cruel, unfeeling boundaries to ensure that she didn't misunderstand the exact tenor of his proposition.

He had told her he wanted a divorce.

He had told her that after tomorrow they would never meet again.

Star's throat constricted. Her wretched body might quicken at one glance from those stunning dark eyes of his, but did he really think she held herself that cheap?

'You don't want me enough…' Even as that impulsive contention escaped her Star tried to bite the words back, for they revealed all too much of her own feelings.

Luc surveyed her steadily, devastating dark eyes fiercely intent. 'How much *is* enough?'

She wanted him on his knees. She wanted him desperate, telling her that never in his life had he experienced such hunger for any woman. If she couldn't get into his mind, it would be the next best thing. Hot colour warmed her cheekbones.

'How much?' Luc repeated huskily.

'M-more…' The current of excitement he generated in her as he moved closer literally strangled her vocal cords.

More? What did that mean? Familiar frustration raked through Luc. He felt like a man trying to capture a dancing shard of sunlight. He felt out of his depth, which infuriated him. He had expected her to grab that offer with both hands. She never looked before she leapt. She was as hot for him as he was for her. He saw it in her, he could *feel* it in her, only this time she was holding back. Star, exercising restraint? Why? What more could he offer?

'Cash inducement?' Luc enquired with lethal cynicism.

Her eyes widened, and then she couldn't help it. A nervous laugh bubbled from her dry throat.

His superb bone structure snapped taut, hooded dark eyes glittering. He reached out a lean brown hand, closed it over her narrow wrist and tugged her close, so close she stopped breathing. 'You think this is funny?'

Belatedly, Star saw that *he* didn't. He thought she was laughing at him, but sheer disbelief had made her laugh. She gazed up into the night-dark depths of his eyes. The wickedly familiar scent of him washed over her. The faint tug of some citrus-based lotion overlaying warm, husky male. She wanted to bury her face in his jacket and breathe him in like an intoxicating drug.

'Not funny...*sad*.' Star struggled to retain some element of concentration even as his raw magnetism pulled at her senses on every level. 'I think you'd prefer it if I asked for money.'

He released his breath in a stark hiss. 'That's rubbish—'

'You could call me greedy then. You could judge me, stay in control.'

'I'm not *out* of control.'

'You like paying for things...you don't value anything that comes free,' Star condemned shakily, fighting not to lean into him.

'*Ciel!*' Luc countered with roughened frustration and impatience. 'Since you and your mother entered my life, everything has had a price!'

At that charge, which had its basis in actual fact, Star paled. Simultaneously from somewhere in the distance there was the most almighty screeching sound, followed by a loud crash. As she jerked back from him, Star's eyes flew wide with dismay.

Luc swung away with a frown. 'What was that?'

Star groaned. 'It sounded like the scaffolding coming down.'

Loosing an impatient expletive in his own language, Luc headed for the door. Star only then recalled that he had parked his car *beneath* the scaffolding surrounding the tower. Pausing this time to thrust her feet into the leather toe-post sandals lying on her bedroom floor, she hurried outside after him.

When she reached Luc's side he was poised in silence, scanning the huge heap of twisted metal framing and rotten splintered wooden panels which had come down on top of his gorgeous sports car. The car was all but buried from view on three sides.

'*Pour l'amour du ciel...*' he ground out in raw disbelief, abruptly springing back into motion to stride towards the still accessible driver's door.

'What are you doing?' Star cried in panic, grabbing his sleeve to hold him back.

'I need my mobile phone!' Luc launched down at her.

'Are you crazy?' Star pointed to the single tier of scaffolding still hanging at a precarious angle above the destruction below. 'That could fall at any minute!'

'*Oui*...I'm crazy.' Luc flung her a grim slashing glance. 'When you last looked into your little crystal pyramid, did you put a *curse* on me?'

Star stiffened until her muscles were as tight as a drum skin. After that derisive response, she resisted the urge to tell him that many people believed in the value of crystal healing. 'There's a phone in the kitchen. You're welcome to use it.'

She walked away, but before she disappeared from sight she stole an anxious glance back. She could see that Luc was still calculating the chance of that last section of scaffolding falling at the exact moment he retrieved his phone from his car.

'Don't you *dare*, Luc Sarrazin!' Star screamed back against the wind, infuriated by his obstinacy, that indefinable male streak which could not bear to duck a challenge.

And in that split second, with a wrenching noise of metallic protest, the remainder of the frame leant outward and came tumbling thunderously down, forcing Luc to back off fast.

Well, that took care of that problem, Star reflected gratefully, and hurried back indoors again.

Luc followed her into the kitchen and approached the huge built-in dresser where the phone sat. 'Who owns this Gothic horror of a dump?' he demanded in a flat tone of freezing self-restraint. 'I intend to sue the owner.'

'Last I heard, Carlton was on a Caribbean island repairing boat engines for the locals. He's poorer than a church mouse,' Star proffered ruefully.

At that news, Luc breathed in so deep she marvelled at the capacity of his lungs. 'That structure was in a very dangerous condition—'

'Yes. An accident waiting to happen.'

His glorious accent was so thick it growled along her nerve-endings like rough tweed catching on the smoothest silk. He was furious, she recognised, outraged by the owner's irresponsibility, not to mention any circumstance which could maroon him in a dilapidated dwelling at the back end of nowhere. She watched him shoot a granite-hard glance of displeasure at his homely surroundings and the strangest feelings began blossoming in Star.

At that instant, Luc was just so human in his fury and his exasperation he provoked a huge melting tide of sympathetic warmth within her. His control over his emotions was so engrained he would not allow himself to shout and storm like most other men would have done. Yet he would be feeling so much less tense and angry if he let himself go. Of course, he wouldn't let himself go, she conceded wryly. But such infuriating events as collapsing scaffolding did not figure much in Luc's life.

He rarely drove himself anywhere. He was a brilliant banker with immense power and influence. A fabulously wealthy but driven workaholic, who had his routine as slavishly organised for him as a prisoner locked up behind bars. His daily existence was smoothed by servants, efficient bank staff, a fleet of chauffeur-driven limos and helicopters and a private jet. In his world of gilded privilege, disaster was invariably kept at a distance, and the irritating, time-consuming repercussions dealt with by someone else.

'I'm really sorry about this...' Star sighed heavily.

Luc lifted a candle to enable him to see the numbers on the phone. 'This is medieval,' he complained with slashing incredulity. 'Did the storm bring down the power supply?'

'No. The lights don't work in here. The whole place needs rewiring, but Carlton can't afford to do repairs. However, the phone's still working.' That was why the original caretaker had moved out, and the only reason why Star had a rent-free roof over her head.

She watched Luc stab out a number on the phone with an imperious forefinger. He'd be calling for another car. When he walked out, she'd *never* see him again. Her thoughts screeched to a bone-jarring halt on that realisation. Like an addict suddenly forced to confront the threatening horrors of denial ahead of her, Star was aghast at that reality. That sense of total loss felt so terribly final she wanted to chain him to the wall, to hold onto him for just a little longer. But she didn't need to chain him, *did* she? He had already offered her a time extension, a little slot, a ridiculously narrow little slot.

Why had he asked her to spend one more night with him? Was it to be his treat or her supposed punishment? My goodness, she thought headily, that one night at the chateau must've been something reasonably acceptable on his terms.

For here was the proof she had never expected to receive. Luc was asking to repeat that night, asking the *only* way he knew how, asking the only way he would allow himself to ask…bargaining from a position of strength and intimidation. Stripping everything bare of emotion, foreseeing every possible future complication but, with a remarkable lack of foresight, risking those same complications. Whooshing tenderness swept over Star like a tidal wave: Luc was acting out of character.

'Why are you looking at me like that?' Luc shot at her with a dark, questioning frown. 'This phone is acting up!'

'It's the storm…put the receiver down and try again,' she advised quietly.

One more night, she bargained with herself. It would be pure and utterly foolish self-indulgence. She would make no excuses for herself. It wasn't sensible, but then loving and wanting Luc Sarrazin had never been sensible. Tomorrow she would *have* to face up to the divorce and the fact that they were like two different planets, forever condemned to spin in separate orbits. Just not meant to be.

Luc was now telling someone at the other end of the line that he wanted a limo to pick him up as soon as possible.

Awkwardly, barely crediting the decision she had reached and instantly terrified that if she lingered on that decision, she might decide against it again, Star cleared her throat, desperate to commit herself.

'*Tomorrow morning…*' she contradicted hoarsely, her mouth feeling as dry as a bone, her tongue too clumsy to do her bidding. 'You won't need the limo until tomorrow morning.'

CHAPTER THREE

LUC was not slow on the uptake.

Tomorrow morning! Star had changed her mind. Or had she? Had she merely been playing games with him all along? His lean, powerful frame tautened. On the phone, his chauffeur was asking for directions. Without any expression at all, Luc gave the details and altered the timing of the arrangement, but his thoughts were already light-years removed from the task at hand. He replaced the receiver in a quiet, controlled movement.

Yet Star tensed like a restive small animal scenting a predator down-wind. As well she might, Luc conceded in febrile abstraction. He wanted to rip her lithe quicksilver body out of those absurd clothes and enjoy the kind of raw, urgent sex he hadn't fantasised about since he was a teenager. But even as the hot blood coursed to his loins, innate caution held him back.

'Tomorrow, we part again.'

'No problem...fresh start for both of us,' Star pointed out shakily.

It was what she needed, Star told herself urgently. The opportunity to draw a final line beneath her disastrous marriage. The chance to rescue a little of her shattered pride at his expense: *he* was the one asking, not she. That was a most ironic first in their relationship. All of a sudden, she had power. He had given her that power. Why shouldn't she use it?

In answer to that defiant question, she tensed as she thought of one very good reason why not for herself. 'Are you involved with anyone else right now?' she asked tightly.

'No,' Luc murmured drily.

Her eyes veiled, Star let her breath slowly escape again. So his mistress, Gabrielle Joly, who had caused her so many sleepless nights of anguish, had finally got her marching orders. Relief quivering through her, she lifted her head again.

Luc was as poised and still as an ice statue, his dark, devastating features unreadable. As he began moving towards her, her heart thumped like a giant hammer inside her.

'Tell me…do you sleep curled up in the hearth here, like Cinderella?' Luc enquired lazily.

'No… Well,' Star qualified tensely, 'I did sleep in here over the winter because my bedroom was too cold.'

He reached for her slowly, as if he was afraid an abrupt movement might startle her into retreat. He wasn't far wrong, Star admitted to herself. Nervous tension already strung her every sinew taut. It had just occurred to her that there was a vast difference between sneaking into Luc's bed when he was asleep…and inviting him to her own bed when he was wide awake and fully in control.

'Luc…?'

'Don't talk…' He lifted a silencing forefinger to trace her parted lips with silk-soft sure delicacy.

She trembled, his merest touch awakening the intense hunger she had fought every day for eighteen months. Aquamarine eyes rested on his lean, dark face with a sudden flare of defiance. 'I won't let you hurt me again—'

'I never meant to hurt you,' Luc ground out, his dark, deep-set eyes flaring to lambent gold.

But how could he have done anything else when he hadn't loved her? He hadn't asked her to love him either, Star reminded herself ruefully.

'It's all in the past,' she swore, as much for her own benefit as his.

Luc curved strong fingers to her exotic cheekbones and tipped her ripe mouth up to his.

As his hands slid down past her slight shoulders to lift her up to him, the sheer power of anticipation made her head

spin in a dizzy whirl. He found her mouth, and for the time-
less space of a heartbeat she lost herself in the hot, hard
hunger of his lips. The most terrifying excitement laced with
undeniable greed currented through her slim body. She linked
her arms round his broad shoulders and pressed herself
against the muscular hardness of his powerful physique, a
fevered gasp of urgency torn from her throat.

He set her down on something hard. She wasn't rational
enough to care what or where. All that motivated her was
the overpowering need to stay physically linked to him. One
kiss and he lit a fever inside her. She burned, heart racing,
pulses pounding, as he dug his fingers into the silky tangle
of her copper hair. He drove his tongue deep in an intimate
invasion as incredibly exciting as it was rawly sexual in intent.

At the height of that explosive passion, Luc dragged his
mouth from hers and gazed down at her with smouldering
heat. *'Diabolique...'* he muttered thickly. 'You're on a table...'

So what? an impatient voice screamed inside her head. As
he lifted his proud dark head bare inches from hers, Star
reached for him with determined hands, sinking her fingers
into the springy black depths of his hair and forcing him back
to her. With a ragged groan of male appreciation, Luc melded
his sensual mouth roughly to hers again, his hands sliding to
the base of her spine to jerk loose the ties of her wrap top.

Hauling her back up into his arms, he lifted his tousled
dark head again, colour scoring the fabulous cheekbones that
lent his face such power. 'Where's the bedroom?'

Star blinked. She was in another world, in which neither
language nor reason existed.

Luc elbowed back the kitchen door. 'Bedroom?'

'First right...*no*, first left!' Every pulse in her treacherous
body was thrumming on a high, making it a challenge to
think.

Luc dipped the tip of his tongue in a provocative flicker

into the tender interior of her mouth, making her jerk with reaction. 'You have the most gorgeous mouth, *mon ange.*'

The sun was going down, intense light flooding through the window to illuminate the small cluttered room. He settled her down on the side of her bed. Her heart was jumping to such an extent she had trouble keeping air in her body. She studied him with passionate intensity. His lean, hard-boned features were half in light, half in shadow. Taut cheekbones, eyes the colour of midnight, straight, arrogant nose, hard, masculine jawline.

She watched Luc cast off his beautifully cut jacket, pull loose his tie and peel off his crisp cotton shirt. He discarded the items with the same controlled cool with which he did everything. Yet she quivered, insidious heat rising from deep within at the sight of his muscular brown chest, the sprinkling of curling black hair hazing his pectorals, the satin-sleek smoothness of the skin over his flat, taut stomach. The strength of her own craving shook her.

'I just love your body,' she whispered, knotting her fingers together, nerves and anticipation headily mingling to keep her ferociously tense.

Luc flashed her a slightly uneasy glance. 'That's my line.'

Star frowned in dismay, taking him literally. 'We don't have to have lines, do we?'

'We don't need to talk, do we?' Evidently even more threatened by that idea, Luc strode forward at speed and raised her upright. The edges of her loosened top fell apart. His hands tightened hard on hers. The silence sizzled. He gazed down fixedly at her bare pouting breasts crested by swollen pink peaks that stirred with her every quickened breath. A tide of colour washed her face as she resisted her own self-consciousness with all her might.

'Sensational...' Suddenly, Luc was dragging the sleeves of her top down her arms, freeing her of the garment and backing her down on the bed with a lack of cool that she found intensely gratifying.

'Say it in French,' she urged breathlessly. 'Say everything in French.'

Momentarily, Luc stilled. 'Try to smother the urge to tell me what to do.'

Star gave him a hurt look of confusion.

He lifted her up against the pillows so that she was level with him. Excitement glanced through her, sharp as a knife, but the pained light in her eyes lingered. He closed a soothing hand over her taut fingers, forcing her to release her death-grip on the corner of the duvet. 'Just keep quiet,' he practically begged. 'Don't talk…when you talk, you drive me crazy.'

Very slowly, Star nodded.

Eyes burning gold swept over her. He snatched in a ragged breath. 'You just always say the wrong thing.'

Tears stung her eyes behind her lowered eyelids.

Luc gazed down at her in frantic frustration. She was lying there like a corpse now, still as death in human sacrifice mode. He curved not quite steady hands to her delicate cheekbones. '*I* always say the wrong thing,' he contradicted in desperation.

Star opened her wonderful eyes and nodded forgivingly.

Without hesitation, he captured her lips again with potent driving passion. She stopped thinking, as if he had punched a switch. He slid lithely down the bed and closed his mouth urgently over one thrusting tender pink nipple. She gasped and jerked, every muscle straining in reaction, and instantly she was on fire again. The tormenting sensitivity of her own flesh made her moan helplessly and melted her quivering body to hot liquid honey.

'I want to taste you…' Luc muttered raggedly, wrenching her out of her skirt, his mouth travelling down over her slim, twisting length with a hot, devastating sensuality that overwhelmed her.

There was no escape from the raw force of her own need. Her heart racing, she flung back her head as he found the hot moist centre of her. A low, keening cry of reaction erupted from her. She was out of her mind with excitement, lost in the domination of an expert sensualist and increasingly frantic as the nagging, terrible ache for fulfilment built ever higher. Her fingernails scored his shoulders in a wild passion of impatience.

'Luc!' she sobbed in despair.

He came over her then, and slid between her trembling thighs. She couldn't get him there quick enough. The fire inside her was all-consuming. He sank into her on one powerful thrust, and the pleasure was so tormentingly intense she almost passed out at the peak of it. Nothing had ever felt so good. And there was more and more and more, and she was hugely desperate to hold onto every sensation and make it last as long as she possibly could. Out of control, she let that mad spiral of tormenting excitement gather her up and send her sobbing and mindless to the intense height of a climax that totally wiped her out.

Afterwards, the first thing she was conscious of was the silence. Luc was still holding her, every damp, hard, muscular line of him welded to her smaller, slighter frame. For a moment she luxuriated in that feeling of intimacy and closeness. Then her mind awakened again, and with a sinking heart she recognised her own weakness.

'Star...' Luc husked in an indolent tone of satiation. 'It's never been like that for me.'

She hoped it never would be again. In fact she hoped she would be a tantalising memory that infuriated him until the day he died. Mustering every scrap of self-discipline she possessed, she forced herself to pull away from him. Unexpectedly, he caught her back to him. In the half-light, dark golden eyes appraised her flushed triangular face, her lowered lashes which betrayed only a wary glimmer of aquamarine.

'You can talk now,' he murmured, almost teasingly.

'I've got nothing to say.' Once she would have told him

she loved him. And that recollection of her old self now made
her cringe.

Luc came up on one elbow, stunning dark eyes level.
'Star—'

'We left the candles burning in the kitchen.' She snaked
out of his hold before he could guess her intention. Stretching
out a frantic seeking hand for the wrap lying on the chair by
the bed, she got up, keen to make her escape.

In the kitchen, she shivered, cold as ice without him, even
colder when she looked into the future. Yet her body still
thrummed and ached from the glorious possession of his.
How dared he make it even better than she had remembered?
How dared he tell her that that was the best sex he had ever
had? He didn't have a sensitive bone in his entire body. But
then what did that matter now?

She felt anguish beckoning like an old friend, but she
turned away from it, older and wiser now. Making a meal of
misery wouldn't change anything. She forced herself to put
away the groceries which Rory had brought. The prosaic task
dragged her down from the heights, gave her the chance to
get a grip on her turbulent emotions.

It was past time that she faced up to the truth she had
spent such an impossibly long time evading. Their marriage
had been a fake! She had known that from the outset but had
stubbornly refused to accept the fact. Luc had never wanted
to marry her; Luc had simply felt that he *had* to marry her,
Star acknowledged painfully.

That winter his father had been dying, Star had enjoyed a
long-awaited and very emotional reunion with her mother.
Only one awkward fact had shadowed that reconciliation:
Juno hated the Sarrazin family and had been desperate to
persuade Star to leave France. But Star had been head over
heels in love with Luc…and quite incapable of choosing to
remove herself from his immediate radius.

On an unannounced visit to the chateau, her mother had
been genuinely appalled to walk into a room and find Star

in Luc's arms. Accusing Luc of taking inexcusable advantage of her teenage daughter's naivety, Juno had threatened to create a major scandal. Determined to protect his sick father from the distress of such sordid publicity, Luc had insisted that they get married. It was ironic that Juno had been even more outraged by their marriage.

But Star had entered their marriage of convenience with a hidden agenda the size of a jumbo jet. She had honestly thought that if she prayed hard enough, tried hard enough, she could *make* Luc love her! Every scrap of misery she had suffered since, she decided, she had brought on herself.

Fortunately, she didn't love Luc any more, she told herself fiercely. He was her first love. It was understandable that she would never be *totally* indifferent to him. But here, tonight, she promised herself that she would say goodbye to that humiliating past and move on. When the dawn came in tomorrow, there would be no looking back.

Having got her flailing emotions back under control, Star drifted back to the bedroom and lodged uncertainly in the doorway, striving for a cool stance. In the moonlight, Luc was lying in a relaxed sprawl on his side, his skin vibrant gold against the pale bedding. He looked like an incredibly gorgeous oil painting. Her heart gave a treacherous lurch. She waited for him to lift his handsome dark head and say something. When he didn't, she moved slowly closer. She couldn't believe it. He had gone to sleep! But then when had Luc *last* slept? She swallowed a rueful laugh, bitterly amused by her own intense disappointment. He followed a relentless schedule. He would have had to make time for a trip to England. To do so he might well have worked through most of last night. And now, tension released by a rousing bout of entirely uncommitted sex, he had given way to exhaustion and fallen asleep. How touchingly, uncharacteristically human! It shocked her that she was really tempted to wake him up again.

Refusing to give way to that degrading desire, Star sat in

the kitchen by the light of one candle. She didn't trust herself to get back into bed with him. She didn't even trust herself asleep in bed with him. Around Luc she did things she would not have dreamt of doing with any other man. Of course this time it was only the lure of his sexual magnetism, his heart-breaking good-looks, his lithe, beautifully built body. In other words, sex—and he was very, very good at sex; that was the only reason she was still tempted...

The limousine arrived at eight the next morning. The chauffeur delivered a garment bag and a small case to the door and then retreated back to the car.

By then Luc was already up, although Star had yet to see him. Minutes earlier she had heard the shower running in the bathroom, and had marvelled at Luc's staying power under that freezing cold gush. Her own record was three minutes, and she always boiled the kettle for hot water to wash her hair. She put the garment bag and the case into the bedroom and went back into the kitchen to wait.

She had already fed the twins and dressed them in their best outfits: Venus in a pink velour top and leggings, Mars in navy dungarees with a checked shirt. They looked cute. At least, Star thought they did. Hopefully, at some stage, a vague memory of the twins looking cute and cuddly would slightly soften the blow of paternity coming Luc's way. When the divorce proceedings began she would have to get a solicitor. She would then tell her solicitor to tell Luc's solicitor that Luc was the father of her twins.

Star could see no reason to confront Luc with the fact that he was a father face to face. Luc was going to be furious. Luc was going to feel trapped and resentful. Luc liked everything to go to plan. Only he hadn't planned on succumbing to her the night she'd sneaked into his bed, and she hadn't planned as far as him actually succumbing, so she hadn't taken any precautions against pregnancy. Why *should* she put herself through a humiliating scene like that? Nothing she could do or say would make the fact of the twins' existence any more palatable to him, she reasoned painfully. It would be much easier all round if he received the news from a third party.

Just then, she heard Luc's steps in the passageway. Her tension level shot so high she felt light-headed. She fixed a really bright and friendly smile to her face. Luc strode through the door as immaculate and elegant as if he had just strolled out of the Sarrazin bank in Paris. Charcoal-grey suit, burgundy silk tie, pale silk shirt. He looked spectacular, and very, very intimidating.

'You should have wakened me earlier,' he drawled smoothly.

Encountering brilliant dark eyes as cool as ice, Star hung on gutsily to her smile. 'Do you want some breakfast?'

'I'm fine, thank you.' Luc glanced at his watch. 'If you're ready, we should leave now for London.'

The horrible silence stretched. But he wasn't touched by it. Or by her discomfiture. She could see that. Inside himself, Luc was already so far from her he might as well have been back in France. There wasn't a hint of warmth or intimacy. There was nothing. It was as if last night had never happened. And Star, who had believed herself prepared for whatever he might choose to throw at her the morning after, just could not cope with that complete denial.

'Do you think I'm going to cling to you now or something?' she heard herself demand rawly.

Luc froze, but on the way to freezing he winced.

Hot-cheeked with fury and pain, Star stepped forward. 'I'm *over* you!' she launched at him.

'We haven't got time for a scene,' Luc murmured deflatingly.

Star trembled, and her hands squeezed into defensive fists. 'Saying how I feel is not creating a scene!'

Luc elevated an aristocratic brow. 'Doesn't it occur to you that I might not be interested in how you feel?'

The angry colour drained from her skin, her expressive eyes shaken.

As Star spun away, Luc gritted his even white teeth. That sunny smile she had greeted him with had filled him with volcanic rage. The Star he remembered would have been self-conscious, shy. Not this one. Involuntarily, he recalled the wild sweetness of her response the night he had consummated their marriage. His body reacted with a surge of fierce arousal, infuriating him.

As a punishment, he made himself focus on the shabby playpen and its tiny occupants. Both babies were watching him with surprisingly intent expressions. The littlest one, with the explosion of copper curls, the colour of which jarred horribly with her pink outfit, gave him a big, gummy winsome smile. That smile was so hopeful and appealing that in spite of the mood he was in he very nearly smiled back. Focusing on the little boy, with his solemn dark brown eyes and slightly anxious air, Luc was astonished to find himself thinking that they were remarkably attractive babies. He looked swiftly away again, but not before he had reminded himself that those children were now *his* responsibility as well. Who else was there to support them?

Star turned back, determined to stand her ground, no matter how much his attitude upset her. 'We had a good time in bed last night. It was just sex. I *know* that,' she told him fiercely. 'But it was my way of saying goodbye to you. I will not be treated like some sleazy one-night stand.'

Luc surveyed her with dark, deep eyes and remained maddeningly silent.

Star squared her slight shoulders. 'Believe it or not, I'm really happy now that we're getting a divorce. I have someone in my life who cares about me and now I'll be free to enjoy that relationship. *He* has a heart, and an imagination…and he talks as well.'

Luc's narrowed gaze chilled her to the bone. The atmosphere seemed to have dropped in temperature to the level of a polar freeze. 'Are you finished?'

Star compressed her lips and spun away, wondering why she had bothered to try and get through to him. 'I'll get the twins' car seats—'

Luc frowned. 'You're planning to bring them with us?'

Star spun back in bewilderment. 'What else would I do with them?'

It was clear that it had not occurred to Luc to wonder what else she might do with the twins. But then in his world young children were invariably in the convenient care of a nanny.

'You just didn't think, did you?' she said witheringly. 'Where I go, Venus and Mars have to go too.'

Luc stilled, his ebony brows drawing together. 'Venus...and Mars?'

'Juno christened them in their incubators.' Star hated the defensive edge she heard in her own voice. 'I know their names sound a little fanciful, and I may have put Viviene and Max on their birth certificates, but Venus and Mars are names which gave them good luck when they really needed it.'

'Venus and Mars,' Luc repeated with a sardonically curled lip.

Cheeks warm with angry colour, Star scooted past him to fetch the car seats from the twins' bedroom. As she emerged, Luc lifted them from her hands with easy strength. 'I'll take these outside.'

As the limousine drove towards London, Star worked hard at not looking in Luc's direction. But she remained agonisingly conscious of his all-pervasive presence. Their relationship, it seemed, had turned full circle. Once again, Luc was taking her to Emilie Auber and then planning to walk out of her life again. Her mind roamed back to their first fateful meeting eleven years earlier...

Her stepfather, Philippe Roussel, had died when she was

nine. In his will he had named Roland Sarrazin as her guardian. Since Philippe hadn't had contact with the Sarrazins since his own childhood, he could only have chosen Luc's father in the hope that the wealthy banker might feel obligated to offer his widow and her child financial help.

By then, Juno and Star had been living on the breadline in Mexico. Philippe had been charming, but hopelessly addicted to gambling. Only after his death had Juno shame-facedly admitted that she had fallen pregnant with Star *before* she'd met Philippe, and that he had not been Star's real father.

Roland Sarrazin had sent Luc to Mexico to track them down. At the time, Juno had been feeling a failure as a mother.

'I had no job, no money, no proper home for you, and you were missing out on your education. I thought that the Sarrazins would take care of you until I got my life sorted out. Then I would bring you back to live with me,' Juno had shared painfully years later, when mother and daughter had finally been reconciled after their long separation. 'How could I ever have dreamt that it would be nine years before I saw you again?'

Juno was still very bitter about that. Roland Sarrazin had applied to a French court to gain full custody of her daughter.

Luc had only been twenty then, but he had had an authority and a maturity far beyond his years. Star had waited outside their shabby one-room apartment while Luc talked to her mother. Within a couple of hours of that meeting Star had found herself accompanying Luc on a flight back to France.

Luc hadn't had a clue how to talk to a child, but he had made a real effort to be kind and reassuring. He had also appeared to believe that she was coming to live with his family, and he had described Chateau Fontaine, their fabulous seventeenth-century home in the Loire valley.

But on their arrival there his father's air of frigid disapproval had frightened and confused Star. Apart from commenting that she was a astonishingly plain little girl, Luc's beautiful mother, Lilliane, had displayed no more interest in her than she might have done in a stray cat.

'My parents are very busy people.' Luc had hunkered down to Star's level to explain when she'd looked up at him with big hurt eyes welling with tears.

'They don't w-want me,' she had sobbed helplessly. 'Why did you bring me here?'

'My father is your legal guardian.'

'What about my mum?'

'Right now your mother can't look after you the way you need to be looked after, and she wants you to catch up with your schooling.'

The following day, Luc had flown her over to Emilie in London. She had been greeted with open arms and home-made lemonade and biscuits.

Of course, how *could* Luc have explained that his father had been outraged at being landed with responsibility for her? A formidably correct man, with immense pride in his own respectability, Roland Sarrazin had had a pronounced horror of scandal. Years earlier, Philippe Roussel had disgraced his own family. The circumstances in which Star and her mother had been living, not to mention the discovery that Star was *not* Philippe's child, had convinced Roland Sarrazin that to protect himself from any further embarrassment he should ensure that Star's mother, Juno, was kept out of her daughter's life.

Emerging from the memory of that cold-blooded and entirely selfish decision, Star glanced at Luc. He had a desk in his limo: that really said it all. He was using a laptop computer while simultaneously talking on the phone. They had shared not a word of conversation since the journey began. The twins, initially eager to attract Luc's attention, had finally given up on him and dozed off.

Star found herself watching the way stray shards of dimmed sunlight flickered through the tinted windows, glinting over the springy luxuriance of his black hair, shadowing a hard cheekbone and accentuating the lush length of lashes longer than her own. One lean brown shapely hand rested on the edge of the desk. Dear heaven, even his hands were beautiful, she thought, suddenly stricken to the heart and sucking in a steadying breath so deep it left her dizzy.

A phone buzzed. Luc lifted his arrogant dark head, a slight frown line etched between his winged brows as he recognised that the phone ringing was not, in fact, his. Star dug into her capacious bag to produce the mobile which Rory had given her for her recent birthday, thinking how unfortunate it was that she had never got the chance to give her mother the number of her mobile phone.

'Star, where *are* you?' Rory demanded anxiously. 'I drove up and saw that car buried under the scaffolding. I was afraid that you'd been hurt!'

'Oh, no, I'm fine…really I am, Rory.' Star smiled with determination, grateful for anything capable of distracting her from Luc's intense visual appeal. Just like the night they had shared, such reactions belonged in the past now, she reminded herself doggedly. It was Rory she should be concentrating on. Rory, who was steady and caring. Rory, who would probably never seek a mistress who resembled a supermodel…

'Luc's taking me to visit Emilie. I was sort of rushed out the door and I forgot to call you.' Star faltered on that last enervating recollection of Gabrielle Joly.

'When will you be home?' Rory prompted.

'Soon…' Looking up to meet Luc's eyes, which were as cold and dark as the river Styx, reputed to lead into the underworld, Star swallowed with difficulty. 'Look, I'll call you when I get back. I'll make a meal,' she proffered on the spur of the moment.

The boyfriend was history, Luc decided without hesitation. A relationship in which neither fidelity nor loyalty appeared to figure was very bad news for Star. And if she couldn't work that out for herself, it was obviously *his* job to do it for her. What Star needed was a fresh start. For that reason, he would make his own generous financial support conditional on Rory's exit from her life. A case of being cruel to be kind. For her own good, and that of her children, Star would have to learn to like a quieter, more conventional lifestyle, he reflected with grim satisfaction.

But she had changed. Last night he had been waiting for her to tell him she still loved him. He could not understand why her failure to do what he definitely hadn't wanted her to do should have irritated the hell out of him. Quite deliberately, Luc dredged up purgative memories of their six-week marriage. Star calling him every hour on the hour…Star reading poetry out loud over breakfast…Star waiting for him every night when he came home, even if it was the next morning…Star, outrageously sensitive and vulnerable but as subtle as an army tank, and yet so loving, so incredibly loving and giving…

His hooded gaze chilled on that final reflection. Over the last eighteen months she had been loving and giving with how many *other* men?

At that moment, the limo pulled in at the tiny mews house where Emilie had lived for over forty years.

'Is Emilie expecting us?' Star asked awkwardly.

'*Bien sûr*…I contacted her before I arrived with you last night.' Luc watched Star lean forward with the evident intention of undoing her daughter's seat restraint. 'Why don't you leave the children sleeping? My chauffeur will watch over them. I don't expect this to be a long visit.'

Star frowned. 'But—'

'Indeed, I imagine that you will be relieved when this meeting is at an end.'

Star stiffened. 'I'm very fond of Emilie. I may be upset and embarrassed about what's happened, but I'm still looking forward to seeing her.'

Luc looked singularly unimpressed by that claim. Star

tilted her chin. Emilie was already waiting at her front door,
a tall, spare woman with soft white hair and a remarkably
fresh complexion for a lady of seventy-two years.

'I was delighted when Luc told me that he would be bringing you with him.' Emilie greeted Star with a warm and
affectionate hug and whispered, 'Thank goodness you've finally told him about the twins.'

While Star reddened at that misapprehension on the older
woman's part, Emilie went to peer into the limo at the slum-
bering babies. 'I do hope they wake up before you have to
leave.'

In the pretty sitting room, Star sat down opposite Emilie.

'I was most annoyed when I found out that my accountant
had dragged you into this, Luc,' Emilie confided, discon-
certing both her visitors.

'I wasn't dragged, Emilie...and Hodgson was only doing
his job.'

'But he completely misread the situation. I *offered* Juno
my money; she didn't ask me for it and she didn't want to
accept a loan from me. I persuaded her to accept my help.
Now that the gallery had failed—through no fault of hers, I
might add—I will not have the poor woman hounded as if
she's a criminal!'

That spirited defence of her mother took Star entirely by
surprise. Luc's dark, devastating features betrayed no reaction whatsoever.

'Juno's a kind and decent woman who's had a very difficult life and more than her fair share of bad luck.' Emilie
proclaimed in determined addition.

Tears stinging her eyes in a hot, emotional surge, Star
reached across and grasped Emilie's hand with very real grat-
itude. 'My mother means well...she always means well...but
nothing ever seems to go right for her,' she agreed shakily.

'Or for anybody else in her vicinity,' Luc completed in a
gritty undertone.

'I *know* that she shouldn't have run away like this,' Star acknowledged tautly, ignoring that comment.

'But Juno didn't run away. She came to see me first.' Emilie's smile of recollection was wry. 'Full of crazy ideas about how she might rescue us both from ruin...bless her heart. She does try *so* hard!'

'Bless...her...heart?' Luc studied his father's elderly cousin much as he might have studied someone intellectually challenged.

'A well-known artist had agreed to exhibit at the gallery opening night,' Emilie explained with a sigh. 'But last month he pulled out. I'm afraid the other artists backed out then too. By then, all the money had been spent on setting up the gallery and funding the advance publicity. It really wasn't her fault.'

'Only Juno could emerge from this fiasco white as driven snow,' Luc commented icily.

Star flinched.

Luc met Emilie's anxious blue eyes and produced a reassuring smile. 'However, I'm relieved that you've not been as upset by this business as I had feared, Emilie. And, believe me, you have nothing further to worry about. As Juno is my mother-in-law, I will naturally replace the money you've lost.'

Emilie frowned. 'I really couldn't allow you to do that, Luc.'

'Of course you could.' Luc did not take that claim seriously.

But, conscious of the level of Emilie's discomfiture, Star was now studying the older woman with questioning concern.

'This is a family matter,' Luc pointed out with impressive conviction.

'*Is it?*' Emilie pursed her lips. 'Families live together and support each other, Luc. But you and Star have been apart for a long time now. In those circumstances, how could I possibly allow you to repay Juno's loan? I can't think of her as your mother-in-law when I know that your marriage must be over.'

A silence in which a dropped pin could have been heard had spread while Emilie explained her reasoning. That the older woman was serious about what she was saying was clear.

Star stole one fleeting glance in Luc's direction. His pronounced stillness suggested that he was as stunned by this development as she herself was. It had not occurred to Luc that Emilie, who invariably agreed with everything he said and did, might flatly *refuse* an offer of financial restitution! And why was Emilie refusing? Emilie believed that their broken marriage meant that she could not consider Juno's debt as being either a family concern *or* Luc's responsibility.

'On the contrary, Emilie,' Luc countered with brilliant dark eyes, a faint smile curving his wide, sensual mouth. 'Our marriage is not over. Star and I were about to tell you that we've just embarked on a trial reconciliation.'

CHAPTER FOUR

LIKE a woman caught up in a sudden polar blast of bone-chilling cold, Star simply froze in position.

Her stunned gaze fixed to Luc's bold, masculine profile while he focused his entire attention on Emilie. *A trial reconciliation?* Star could not credit her own ears! Luc was famed for his ice-cool nerves and fast reactions in times of crisis. How could a male as clever, cautious and controlled as Luc have made such an insane announcement?

'That is the most wonderful news I've ever heard!' With a sudden smile of surprise and pleasure, Emilie scrambled up to clasp Luc's hand and extend her other hand expectantly in Star's direction.

'Star...' Luc prompted, in probably much the same commanding tone he employed with slow-moving junior employees at the Sarrazin bank.

But Star stared at Emilie's extended hand and found she simply couldn't move a muscle. Of course, she knew what Luc was *trying* to do. She understood why he had suddenly pulled that whopping fib like a rabbit out of a magician's hat. But how did Luc think that such an enormous lie could be carried off? Pretending that they were having another go at their marriage would demand far more of a convincing show than Luc could fondly imagine.

No doubt he thought he was telling a little white lie which he could easily shrug off again with a regretful sigh at some stage in the future. But then he wasn't aware that Emilie and Star had remained in too close contact for such a pretence to work. And Star was furious at the idea that she might be forced to stay out of touch with Emilie to support that same pretence!

Star collided unwarily with Luc's intimidating dark gaze. Get up and play your part, that hard, warning scrutiny urged. When she failed to move, he bent down and closed his other hand over hers to literally *lift* her up into doing his bidding.

'I'm so very happy for you both.' Emilie folded Star into her arms. 'Although,' she added hesitantly, 'I'm not quite sure I like the sound of that word "trial", Luc. Particularly with young children involved—'

Star jerked back into life and interrupted the older woman by pressing a harried kiss to her cheek. 'I'm so sorry, but we really do have to rush off now, Emilie. You know what Luc's schedule is like! I hope you'll allow Luc to sort out this financial thing for you.'

'Of course Emilie will,' Luc asserted.

'Yes, and then I shall visit you all in France this month,' Emilie announced with an even brighter smile of anticipation, seeming not to notice that Star's expressive face fell by a mile in shock. 'Now I can really look forward to spending the summer at Chateau Fontaine with Star and those beautiful little children of—'

'Gosh, got to run…love you so much, Emilie. See you soon!' Star carolled wildly, yanking on Luc's hand with desperate determination to drag him out of the room before the older woman could spill the beans about the twins' parentage.

Shell-shocked by the experience of visiting Emilie when Luc was in an inventive mood, Star climbed back into the limo and just sat there like a stone effigy, her bemused dismay as to how Emilie's expectations could possibly be met etched in her face.

'We'll fly back to France this evening,' Luc drawled without skipping a beat.

A faint frown line indented Star's smooth brow. 'Sorry…you said…?'

'You heard what I said,' Luc informed her drily.

'I'm *not* coming to France just because you've landed us

in a heck of a mess with that stupid lie!' Star exclaimed in vehement accusation.

Faint colour darkened the superb angles of Luc's hard cheekbones. 'Scarcely a "stupid lie", *mon ange*. It was the only option left. If Emilie won't allow me to repay that money, she'll be homeless by the end of the month. Without the income from the investments she cashed in she can't even pay the rent on that house, never mind hope to keep herself with the smallest degree of comfort!'

Star had paled as he spelt out those harsh facts. 'But—'

'Just for once…concentrate that brain of yours,' Luc advised grimly. 'Your mother reduced Emilie to this level. Emilie's very proud, and she might be talking very bravely at the moment. But at her age how do you think she will cope with such a drastic change in lifestyle? Worry and distress will affect her health and will most definitely shorten her life.'

Star lost even more colour. And by the time Luc had finished speaking she saw that there *were* no other options. Just as suddenly she felt as if she was in a trap. She loved Emilie; she loved Emilie very much. But it seemed awesomely cruel to Star that she should be forced into such a situation on the very day she had finally mustered the sense and courage to say goodbye to Luc and her feelings for him for ever.

'You can spend the summer at Chateau Fontaine,' Luc continued levelly. 'It will be a small price to pay for Emilie's peace of mind. I will stay in the Paris apartment and make occasional weekend visits. Emilie will soon see for herself that you are being sadly neglected. She'll be disappointed, but I'm sure she'll understand when you decide that you *do* want a divorce.'

'Magic…not only do I get to spend three months away from my boyfriend…but I also get to be the one who demands the divorce. Thanks, but no thanks!' Her bright eyes shimmered with angry pain. 'You'll have to come up with something an awful lot better than that!'

Luc dealt her a cool, considering appraisal, dark eyes diamond-bright. 'So you'll have to do without sex for three months. You'll live.'

Star shivered with sheer rage.

'Let me be even more frank,' Luc continued in a tone as smooth as cut-crystal. 'Your life is a disaster zone. You're only twenty and already you have two children. Where's their father?'

Eyes aflame with defiance, Star stared back at him.

'Do you even know who the father is?' Luc drawled.

Furious colour lashing her cheekbones, Star snatched in a ragged breath to steady herself. She wanted to shout back at him, but she didn't want to waken the twins and distress them. 'How dare you ask me that?'

Unmoved, Luc raised a winged brow. 'Is that a yes or a no?'

'Of course I know…and I deeply resent the suggestion that I might *not* have known!' Star dragged her attention from him and focused instead on Venus and Mars. 'But they weren't conceived in what you might call a lasting relationship—'

'You had a one-night stand,' Luc assumed in derisive interruption.

Star breathed in so deep she wondered that she didn't simply explode. 'Yes, I suppose that *would* be the most apt description,' she conceded unevenly. 'The twins weren't planned—'

'So they just happened along, much like you did yourself? Doesn't that strike you as a very irresponsible attitude?'

'Their father was irresponsible too,' Star pointed out dulcetly. 'And the reason he's not helping me to support the twins is that he doesn't know that I got pregnant because I decided not to tell him.'

Luc shifted a broad shoulder. The slight, elegant Gallic shrug of dismissal suggested his waning interest in the subject.

Cut off in full swing, and feeling incredibly snubbed by his apparent lack of normal human curiosity, Star thrust up her chin. 'I can't fly to France this evening.'

'You must,' Luc contradicted. 'You can pack what you need for tonight. I will have the rest of your possessions cleared and flown over tomorrow. We can't afford to appear lukewarm about our reconciliation at this stage.'

'It just gets worse and worse...' Star groaned. 'We're getting sucked deeper and deeper in.'

'I'm afraid there won't be time for you to cook for Rory.' Without the slightest warning, Luc's wide mouth curved into a startlingly charismatic smile.

Her heart jumped like a bemused bird smashing itself against a windowpane. That so rare smile stole her breath from her throat and sent her treacherous pulses pounding. Her colour fluctuating, she collided unwarily with stunning dark eyes alight with amusement, and her sense of impending tragedy simply mushroomed. Her whole body was taut as a bow, every muscle so tight it hurt, and all Luc had done was smile, filling her with intense awareness of his masculinity and all the raw-edged emotions she had sworn to put behind her.

'Unless you've been polishing up your catering skills since we last met, Rory may well live to be grateful for the cancellation,' Luc extended silkily.

At that explanatory reference to an incident from their own past, Star's over-taxed emotions responded by simply flooding her eyes with tears. 'You are *so* insensitive!'

'After last night, I could hardly be expected to appreciate that you are *that* keen on the guy,' Luc murmured with cool, contemptuous clarity.

Humiliated by that rejoinder, Star's hands knotted into fists and she twisted her bright head away, fighting to get herself back under control. He could think what he liked! And as usual he'd read her wrong! Eighteen months ago, in one of her many attempts to persuade Luc to see her as a proper wife, she had given the chateau chef a night off and made dinner one evening. And it had been an absolutely mortifying total fiasco. Anything that hadn't been overcooked had been undercooked. And, worst of all, Luc had attempted to eat those pathetic edible offerings because he'd felt sorry for her.

'My chauffeur will take you home to pack and bring you to the airport in time for the flight this evening,' Luc drawled some minutes later.

Startled by that announcement, Star glanced up and registered that the limousine had already drawn to a smooth halt outside the Sarrazin bank in central London.

'I have several appointments to keep.' His brilliant dark deep-set eyes were cool as ice. 'But, as requested, I've come up with a better explanation with which to satisfy Emilie when our charade of a marriage disintegrates all over again. On this occasion, you can just tell her the truth!'

Star studied him in bewilderment. 'Sorry, I—'

'Did you really think that I wouldn't work out that Emilie appears to believe that your children are *mine*?' Luc demanded with sardonic bite.

Since Star had been guilty of thinking exactly that, she was taken entirely by surprise. A split second later, she found she could not meet his hard, challenging gaze either. Her own shrinking reluctance to tell him the truth about the twins had created this particular misunderstanding.

'You never think anything through to its likely conclusion,' Luc said very drily.

In this particular case he was undeniably correct, and Star was stung. 'How did you guess?' she heard herself asking.

'Emilie would not have welcomed your children had she not believed that I was their father,' Luc pointed out.

And, once again, he was quite right, Star acknowledged with gritted teeth. Had the twins been the result of an extra-marital affair, Emilie Auber would have been very distressed by their birth. Nor, in such circumstances, would she have been so willing to believe the story of their supposed reconciliation.

'Whatever lies you employed to persuade her into crediting that cosy little fiction are your own responsibility,' Luc continued. 'But let me warn you now that while I appreciate the shock which Emilie will suffer when you admit the truth, I won't allow that lie to stand even temporarily in my own home. No matter what discomfiture it causes you, I have no intention of playing along with that particular pretence.'

Star scanned his lean, strong face with sudden aghast intensity. 'But everyone will think I'm a real tart!'

'You said it,' Luc murmured with lethal cool.

Pulverised by that final comment, and furious at herself for giving him that opening, Star watched him swing out of the car with predatory grace and stride towards the entrance of the London headquarters of the Sarrazin bank. Somewhat belatedly, it occurred to her that she had been foolish to allow Luc to continue believing that their children had been fathered by another man, foolish to place her own pride ahead of what was, after all, an unalterable fact. And the sooner she told Luc the truth now the better.

When Star boarded the Sarrazin private jet, she was clutching a squirming Venus under one arm and a clinging Mars under the other. Her floaty blue skirt and white cropped top were sticking to her damp skin. After rushing through the airport, she was feeling really harassed.

Luc strode out to greet her. Sheathed in a formal navy pinstripe suit embellished with a silk geometric print tie, he looked shockingly sexy. A guilty little tremor ran down her backbone.

'Do you realise how long we've been waiting for you?'

Her backbone became suddenly less sensitive. 'I'm sorry.'

She could have bitten her tongue out as soon as she said it. Unfortunately, Emilie had trained her too well, to always apologise for being late. However, Star had had a very difficult afternoon. With no prior preparation, packing for herself and the twins and closing up Highburn Castle had been serious hard work.

She had phoned Rory as soon as she'd got home. He had arrived while she was still struggling to get organised. He had been shattered when she'd told him that she was flying back to France with Luc. While she had still been trying to explain Emilie's financial situation, he had walked out in a temper. Now she could not imagine how she had ever thought she could hold onto *any* kind of relationship with Rory when Luc had stolen her life and her freedom for months to come.

'Who disabled the car phone?' Luc enquired glacially.

'I did.' Star owned up straight off. 'I told you we were stuck in a traffic jam. I didn't see the point of five-minute bulletins.'

Luc breathed in very deep. A combination of relief and raw exasperation powered through him. Punctual to a fault himself, he found her laid-back attitude infuriating. Star could leave a room promising to be *just* five minutes and then forget to come back at all. She was very easily distracted. But when telephone contact with the limousine had abruptly been severed, Luc's stress level had rocketed. He had wondered if Star had changed her mind about their arrangement and gone for the sort of sudden vanishing act her flighty mother excelled at.

'Do you think you could offer to take one of the twins for me?' Star prompted as the ache in her arms at the combined weight of the babies reached an unbearable level.

'Take one of the...?' Luc just froze.

Star shifted closer and indicated Venus with a downward motion of her chin.

'Where do I take hold of it?' Luc demanded.

'Just grab her before I drop her!' Star urged.

Luc clasped Venus between two stiff hands and held his daughter in mid-air like an unexploded bomb. Initially delighted by the transfer, Venus then picked up on that adult uncertainty and let out an anxious wail of fright. In response, Luc extended his arms to put an even greater distance between them. Venus squirmed and yelped in panic, clearly thinking she was on the way to being dropped.

'Hold her close, for goodness' sake...you're frightening the life out of her!' Banding both her arms round Mars, Star sighed with relief at the easing of the strain in her muscles.

Luc grated, 'I've never held a baby before!'

'Well, it's about time you learned. Babies are very touchy-feely and like to know they're secure.' Out of the corner of her eye, she watched Luc draw Venus closer with such pronounced reluctance she could have kicked him.

'Why's she going all slack?' Luc enquired in a driven undertone.

'Because she's in cuddle mode.' She watched Venus snuggle her curly head down on Luc's shoulder and just sag, the way very tired babies do.

'She's got little bones like a bird,' Luc drawled flatly. 'I was afraid I might hurt her.'

In the luxurious working area which made up only about a sixth of the passenger space available on the extensive Sarrazin jet, Star settled Mars into one of the baby seats awaiting occupancy. Luc bent down for her to peel Venus off his shoulder.

'Cots have been organised for them in the rear cabin,' Luc advanced.

Star strapped herself in beside the twins. Minutes later, the powerful jet taxied towards the runway. Luc was already perusing a file at the far side of the cabin. Star suppressed a rueful laugh. She had planned to tell Luc during the flight that Venus and Mars were his *own* flesh and blood. But she was exhausted, and what difference would another few hours make? She would be calmer and better equipped to deal with making that announcement in the morning.

As soon as they were airborne, the stewardess approached her and showed her down to the rear cabin, mentioning that a meal was about to be served, but Star said that she wasn't hungry. Having settled Venus and Mars into the cots, she decided to take advantage of the bed beside them and get some rest.

About ten minutes later, the door opened with quiet care. 'You should eat something,' Luc informed her levelly.

Half asleep, Star flipped over, copper hair tumbling over one exotic cheekbone, aquamarine eyes heavy. Light spilled in from the passage to glimmer over the satin-smooth skin of her slender waist where the crop-top had ridden up. As she stretched unselfconsciously, the extended length of one long shapely leg emerged from the folds of her skirt.

She studied Luc from below her dark lashes, the perceptible tension in the atmosphere tugging at her senses.

'You look like a gipsy,' Luc murmured.

The dark, deep pitch of his accented drawl quivered along her nerve-endings, awakening treacherous warmth low in the pit of her stomach.

'*Sauvage*…wild,' he breathed in husky addition.

Suddenly her every muscle was taut. She stared helplessly at him. So tall, so dark, so extravagantly, breathtakingly gorgeous. Hunger surged up inside her with such greedy immediacy she could barely breathe. In a split second she relived the urgent passionate force of his sensual mouth only just over twenty-four hours earlier, the hard, powerful pressure of his expert body moving on and in hers. Sensual weakness cascaded like melting fire through her, her breasts now full and swelling, their pointed peaks tightening into aching prominence. But then, just as suddenly, she remembered how Luc had behaved after he had got out of her bed. Cool, distant, dismissive, all intimacy forgotten.

Star lifted her bright head from the pillow, aquamarine eyes glinting now with angry self-loathing. 'Wild…but not free…not free to you *ever* again,' she told him.

Luc surveyed her with glittering intensity. 'This has the feel of a negotiation—'

'*Ever* the banker,' Star heard herself chide, but she was on a high from the excitement electrifying the atmosphere, a high that increased to the level of a stunning power surge when Luc bent the entire force of his concentration on her.

'The situation has changed—'

'Has it?' Star let her head tip back, soft, full mouth in a slight considering pout. 'I don't think so. I just think you always want what you believe you shouldn't have. But leave me out of it. It'd cost you too much.'

'*How* much?'

'Your problem is that you can't think of cost except in terms of money,' Star sighed without surprise, knowing that he would definitely run a mile if he suspected that further intimacy might well persuade her to stick like glue to him and refuse a divorce for as long as she could.

Luc dragged in a roughened breath.

'And anyway,' Star purred, like a little cat flexing her claws as she sent him a sidewise languishing glance, 'I'm not tall *or* blonde *or* sophisticated. So we can't possibly have a problem, can we?'

Without the slightest warning, Luc bent down and hauled her slight figure all the way up into the strong circle of his arms. A startled gasp of disbelief was wrenched from Star. He welded her into every angle of his hard, masculine physique and crushed her soft mouth with savage hunger under his. He stole every scrap of air from her quivering body. Burning fire leapt up at the very heart of her, a sweet, desperate ache stirring to make her slender thighs tremble.

Luc lowered her very gently down onto the bed again. Before he left, he scanned her flushed and bemused face with slumbrous amusement. 'It's not a problem for me, *mon ange*.'

He was right; it was *her* problem, Star acknowledged in shaken honesty. He had shot her to the height of excitement so fast she was still reeling from the extent of her own weakness. She hadn't realised that her limited ability to resist Luc

might be tested again. Only now did she see that in acceding
with such apparent ease to Luc's request that she spend one
last night with him she had given him entirely the wrong
impression. About her, about her attitude to sex...

Indeed, the very *worst* impression that she could have
given him now that they were pretending to be reconciled
for Emilie's benefit! Star cringed, embarrassed and angry
with herself when it was far too late to change anything. Luc
assumed that what she had done with such seeming casual-
ness *once* she would surely be eager to do again. And evidently Luc was more than willing to take advantage of any
such eagerness on her part. Yet that reality left Star in even
deeper shock. Luc was *finally* awarding her adult status, but
only in the most basic field a woman could qualify in.

But their marriage was over, and she didn't believe in casual sex. The night before, she had genuinely been saying
goodbye to Luc and her love for him. But a male as unemo-
tional as Luc couldn't possibly understand such reasoning.
He had simply noted that his soon-to-be-ex-wife had dem-
onstrated little reluctance to jump into bed with him again.
In fact they might never have got beyond the kitchen had it
been left up to her. So why didn't she just face the ugly truth
head-on? Luc now thought she was not much better than a
tart...

Didn't say much for *his* morals, did it? Naively, she would
have believed that Luc would be too fastidious to want a
woman who might make herself so freely available to men.
Just showed how much she knew about his sex! Just showed
how much she knew about the man she had married!
Suddenly, Star was in a white-hot rage with Luc, and very,
very grateful that they would be getting a divorce...

As the limousine travelled down the thickly wooded approach road to Chateau Fontaine, Mars finally fell asleep
again.

Star could have wept at her son's sense of timing. Mars

had cried from the minute he was rudely removed from his cosy cot on board the Sarrazin jet. He had wailed like a howl alarm all the way through Nantes Atlantique airport. Working himself up into a state of inconsolable misery, he had kept his mother far too busy to worry about anything else.

But now, when she finally had the peace to consider the timing of the trip which she and the twins had been forced to make, her resentment overflowed. 'Mars will probably be crying half the night.'

Luc elevated a winged brow, a perceptible air of self-satisfaction in his level dark gaze. 'I doubt it. I have an extremely competent nanny awaiting the children at the chateau.'

Star's jaw dropped.

'I should have asked Bertille to meet us at the airport—then we might all have enjoyed a more relaxing trip.'

Star's jaw would have hit the floor had it had not been securely attached to other bones. 'I don't believe I'm hearing this. *You*—'

Luc frowned. 'What's wrong?'

'What's *wrong*?' Star gasped incredulously. 'You organise a nanny, over the top of my head…then you suggest that *she* could've managed my son better than I have!'

Registering his error as the limo filtered to a halt in front of the chateau, Luc shifted a fluid hand, intended to soothe Star. 'You misunderstood me—'

'Did I heck!' Star shot back at him fiercely. '*You're* the one responsible for my son's distress—'

'If you don't keep your voice down, you're likely to wake him up again,' Luc countered in icy warning just as the passenger door beside Star swung open with a thick, expensive clunk.

'Who was it who *insisted* on travelling with two babies until this hour of the night?' Star demanded. 'Of course Mars has been upset. All he wants is to be home in his *own* snug little cot—'

'In a building which should be condemned, "snug" is scarcely the most apt word! Your so-called *home* is unfit for human habitation!'

Pained condemnation filled her disconcerted gaze. 'I didn't notice you being half so fussy last night!'

As she spoke, Luc noticed the passenger door standing wide. He frowned like a male emerging from a dream, his lean, dark devastating features setting into unyielding lines. The chauffeur was nowhere to be seen, presumably having decided that desertion of his duties was more tactful than hovering to listen to the happily reunited couple having a thunderous row.

His brilliant eyes glimmered like a banked-up fire ready to flame. 'I suggest we drop the subject. There's no reason for this dispute. It is irrational—'

'Irrational? You insulted me. You, who can't even hold a baby for five seconds without panicking, *dared* to deride my maternal abilities,' Star enumerated shakily as she tugged Venus out of her car seat. 'You insulted me, my home, my hospitality. Yet it was your arrogant refusal to rearrange your schedule, your stupendous ignorance of childcare, your absolute conviction that everybody has to jump to do exactly what you want when you want which was at fault.'

'If you don't keep quiet, I will treat you like a child having a temper tantrum, because that is how you are behaving,' Luc condemned with freezing restraint.

'How difficult it must be to deal with someone who has no respect for you, no fear of you and no dependence on your good will. Yes, I can see it must be a real challenge when someone like me dares to fight back. What are you doing with Mars?'

Emerging from the limo in a state of frozen fury, Luc pressed a shielding hand to the baby's back, where he was now carefully draped over Luc's shoulder still fast asleep. 'He's a sensitive child. He doesn't need to be swung about like a little sack of potatoes.'

Star's frown of surprise that he had lifted Mars faded at that point. Her attention was finally grabbed and held by the sheer vast magnificence of the building before them. The Chateau Fontaine was illuminated by what appeared to be around a hundred lights, both outside and inside. On her last visit, Star absently recalled how Emilie had strictly warned her not to leave on any unnecessary lights as her guardian paid close attention to all matters which related to household expenditure.

'Of course, Emilie would never have said it, wouldn't even *think* such a disrespectful thing about any member of your illustrious family,' Star found herself musing out loud.

'What are you talking about?' Luc demanded as they crossed the superb arched seventeenth-century bridge that led to the huge and imposing front door.

'Your father was as rich as Croesus, but he was as tight with his wealth as any miser,' Star reflected. 'That's so sad. His only real enjoyment in life seemed to be saving money.'

It was perfectly true, but it had never, ever been said to Luc's face before.

'I suppose he'd have been apoplectic if he'd ever seen all these lights blazing...' Star drifted into the chateau without a backward glance.

Bertille, the nanny, was young and warm and wonderfully appreciative of the twins. Only the meanest and most possessive of mothers could have objected to her assistance, Star conceded ruefully. A bedroom on the first floor had been rearranged as a nursery, and neither Venus nor Mars wakened again as they were settled into comfortable cots. As Bertille was to sleep in the adjoining dressing room, Star said goodnight and wandered back out into the corridor.

It was after midnight, and she was embarrassed to find the housekeeper had been patiently waiting for her to reappear. Self-conscious with such personal attention and the assurance that her humble wardrobe of clothing had already been unpacked for her, Star stiffened uneasily every time she was addressed as a married woman. Even so, it was quite a shock when the older woman opened the door of Luc's bedroom and stood back, leaving Star little choice but to enter.

For the duration of their six-week long marriage, Luc had left her in a bedroom at the foot of the corridor. It had not occurred to Star that anything might be different this time around, but then she really hadn't had time to consider the ramifications of returning to the chateau as Luc's acknowledged wife. One of the bedrooms *next* to his, she decided, would be the most suitable choice.

However, sooner than be seen walking straight back out again, Star lingered. The vast and magnificent room was centred on the superb gilded four-poster bed which sat on a shallow dais. Luc had slept in that incredible bed since he was eight years old. And so might a medieval merchant prince have lived, with glorious brocade drapes, fabulous paintings and the very finest antique furniture.

'Luc was never like other children,' Emilie had once confided. 'He was a very serious little boy.'

But what else could he have been? An only child, born to parents who had inhabited different wings of the chateau and led entirely separate lives.

Lilliane Sarrazin had died in a car crash shortly after Star had met her. Reading between the lines of Emilie's uncritical description, Luc's mother had been as committed to extravagance as her husband had been to saving, but had shared his essentially cold nature. Was it any wonder that Luc, with every natural instinct stifled in childhood, should be so reserved, so controlled, so inhibited at showing either affection or warmth?

And yet Star could remember times when Luc had broken through his own barriers for *her* benefit. He had comforted her when she was nine years old and missing her mother. He had done so again—fatally—when she was eighteen and a half…

Star's memories slowly slid back over eighteen months to

her last stay at Chateau Fontaine. Emilie, who could not bear to think badly of anybody, had worked hard to give Star the impression that Luc's terminally ill father was really a caring man, whom she had misjudged at their only previous encounter. It had not been the wisest idea.

Shortly after her arrival with Emilie, Star had been summoned to her guardian's sick room for a private meeting.

'You've done very well out of this family.' Roland Sarrazin regarded her with sour disapproval.

'I really appreciate everything that you've done for me—'

'Just be grateful that Luc took pity on you,' the older man urged. 'I had no intention of accepting you as my ward when I sent Luc to Mexico. But when he met your mother she was so drunk she could barely stand. Decency demanded that I do my duty by you.'

Devastated by that cruel, demeaning candour, Star spoke up in an angry defensive rush. 'My mother was really dreading giving me up that day. She was terribly upset...it *wasn't* normal for her to be like that!'

'Your stepfather was a weak, pathetic wastrel. You have no idea who your father is and your mother *is* a drunk,' Roland Sarrazin repeated with crushing distaste and contempt. 'With a sordid, shameful background of that kind, how *dare* you raise your voice to me?'

Humiliated and distressed by that counter-attack, Star fled. She ran into the woods that surrounded the chateau to find the privacy to cry. Nine years earlier, Luc had taken her down to the riverbank there to tell her about Emilie and stress how very lonely and sad Emilie had been since losing her husband. Indeed, so successful had he been at impressing Star with those facts that she had been a lot older before she'd appreciated what a huge debt she owed to the older woman.

And, nine years later, somehow Luc knew exactly where to find Star that evening. An hour earlier she had watched his helicopter flying in, had known that soon she would be missed, but she hadn't been able to face the prospect of sitting down to dinner with Luc and Emilie and whoever else might be staying in the vast house.

A Ferrari pulled up on the estate road that ran to within yards of the river. Fresh from a day of high-powered wheeling and dealing at the Sarrazin bank in Paris, Luc climbed out, his appearance one of effortless elegance and supreme sophistication in a beautifully cut charcoal-grey suit.

Nothing could have prepared Star for that first emotional meeting with Luc Sarrazin that winter. Luc, with the remote air of self-containment which surrounded him like an untouchable aura. As he moved with fluid grace towards her, arrows of pale sunlight broke through the overhanging canopy of trees to illuminate his stunning dark deep-set eyes. For Star, it was like being struck by lightning.

He looked so extravagantly gorgeous that he simply took her breath away.

'My father is very ill,' Luc drawled tautly. 'Confined to the sick room as he now is, his temper has suffered. Unfortunately, he tends to lash out at those least able to defend themselves. I must offer you my apologies—'

'Your father despises me…he thinks I'm the lowest of the low!'

'That is not true,' Luc countered with impressive conviction.

And Star sensed how very much Luc wanted her to accept that unlikely assurance and, even more crucially, how *very* difficult he found it to set aside his forbidding reserve and attempt to both explain and apologise for the episode in as few words as possible.

'My mother is *not* a drunk!' Star protested in driven continuance as she moved closer in open and desperate appeal for his agreement. 'And my stepfather may have been a gambler but he was a lovely, lovely man!'

Luc studied her with a tension he could not conceal. 'You touch my conscience. Had I been less frank with my father when I brought you back from Mexico, you might not have been deprived of your mother for so long.'

'No, that wasn't your fault. You didn't know her; of course you got the wrong idea... But that was the *one and only* time I ever saw her drink like that...' Star sobbed as her turbulent emotions overcame her again.

Luc reached out and put his arms round her, very, very slowly, like a newly blind man needing to feel his way with care and caution. There was still a good foot of clear space between them. Star swiftly closed that space. He was as rigid at that physical contact as a living, breathing rock.

'I think it's time you had the opportunity to get to know your mother again,' Luc murmured.

Gently peeling her from him, Luc opened up the space again, but lost his ascendancy as Star flung herself back close and gazed up at him with wondering eyes of hope. 'You actually *know* where Juno is?'

'I do.'

'But how can you?'

'You're eighteen. Strictly speaking, you're no longer my father's ward. If you want to see your mother, I will arrange it.'

'You really mean it?'

'I don't make promises I can't keep.'

And that was the moment when Star fell head over heels in love with Luc Sarrazin. The moment when she pictured how her infinitely less inhibited nature might magically mingle in a perfect match with his. The moment when Luc Sarrazin, temptingly packaged with the hidden vulnerability of his utterly miserable, loveless childhood, became nothing short of an overwhelming obsession for Star.

She only saw Luc being incredibly kind and considerate of her needs. She didn't know that it was imperative Luc ensured that she forgave his father's behaviour and stayed on at the chateau. Why? Roland Sarrazin enjoyed Emilie's restful companionship. Had Star insisted on returning to London,

Luc wasn't convinced that he could depend on family loyalty to keep Emilie in France.

As a door closed softly shut behind her, Star was shot back to the present. She was bemused to find herself still standing in Luc's huge bedroom where, on the night of the twins' conception, she had crept round removing lightbulbs from the lamps to create a more intimate atmosphere. The memory made her cringe.

'I thought you would've been in bed by now,' Luc drawled with the most staggering lack of expression. He said it lightly, casually, as if they had been sharing a bedroom for years.

Star spun round. Her brow furrowed, her eyes bewildered as she ran that sentence back through her brain. 'You think I'm going to sleep in here...with *you*?'

A very faint smile tugged at the edges of Luc's wide, sensual mouth. 'Why so shocked?'

CHAPTER FIVE

STAR gaped at Luc, aquamarine eyes at their widest. She could not credit that he could actually expect her to share a bedroom with him.

'No more drama, *please...*' Luc urged with soft, silken derision as he loosened his well-cut jacket and shrugged out of it to stroll in the direction of the dressing room.

'We'd both be very uncomfortable in the same room!' Star folded her arms together in a jerky movement. 'I'll use one of the rooms next door—'

'*J'insiste,*' Luc responded very, very quietly.

The sheer appalling arrogance of that assurance that he would not take no for an answer shook Star. 'It's quite unnecessary for us to—'

Brilliant dark eyes cool as ice, Luc swung back from about thirty feet away and moved back towards her at a leisurely pace that was oddly intimidating. '*Ecoutes-moi...*listen to me,' he commanded with natural authority. 'As I will not be here very often this summer, the very least we can do in support of this charade is occupy the same room. When it is time to demonstrate waning enthusiasm for that intimacy, you can move out, but *not* before that point.'

'Emilie would never dream of enquiring into our sleeping arrangements!' Star argued.

'But she will certainly notice them. I am not a demonstrative man. I am no actor,' Luc disclaimed with growing impatience. 'That we sleep in the same bed is likely to be the *sole* evidence she sees of our supposed reconciliation!'

Star's chin came up. 'I'd rather settle for you bringing flowers home on Friday evenings. Surely even you could manage that!'

Luc sent her a gleaming glance. 'The flowers are your department. I got a dozen red roses every day of the six weeks we were together. They were delivered to the very door of my office with cute little handwritten cards attached. My staff took extraordinary steps to get the chance to read those cards before I did. Surely you don't think I could have forgotten that experience?'

A crimson blush now flamed over Star's taut cheekbones.

'Should you be thinking of repeating that romantic gesture, do you think it would be possible for you to put the cards into sealed envelopes?'

Fury and intense mortification were licking like flames through Star's slender length. 'Don't worry about it...I'll never ever send you flowers again!'

'And while we're on the subject, you're not getting my mobile phone number until you assure me that it will only be used in an emergency.'

'I've grown out of any desire to keep hourly tabs on your whereabouts!' Star bit out between gritted teeth, eager to escape the dialogue and turning away. 'Well, if I'm going to be stuck in here with you, I'm sleeping on the sofa.'

Luc surveyed the gilded sofa which had been in the family since the late eighteenth century. He said nothing. He knew a marble slab would have offered as much comfort.

Star stalked into the dressing room and rattled and banged through loads of drawers and closets before she found her own small stock of clothing. Gathering up nightwear, she headed for the bathroom. Stripping off her clothes with trembling hands of angry frustration, she switched on the shower. She yelped as enervating jets of water hit her tense body from all directions. Her hair soaked, she threw herself down on the seat in the corner. It was typical of Luc to have a shower with more confusing controls than a rocket ship!

She pictured him as she had last seen him in the bedroom. Tailored silk shirt partially unbuttoned to show a riveting triangle of golden brown skin, taut, flat stomach, lean hips and long hard thighs encased in charcoal-grey trousers cut to enhance every lithe masculine line of his tightly muscled length. A treacherous burst of warmth low in her belly made her tense up even more. She clenched her teeth, hating herself for being so weak. She'd stood there arguing with him and burning for him at the same time. It was sick, indecent.

But Luc had always made her feel like that. Everything about him pulled at her senses, awakening the most tormenting hunger. His dark, deep voice, his husky accent, his beautiful eyes, his sexy mouth. She listened, she looked, she went weak at the knees with lust. *Lust*. She latched onto that word with intense relief. It definitely wasn't love any more; it was lust. A greedy, mindless, wicked craving which she *had* to control, stamp on, stamp *out*!

No longer did she crave that rare smile, that devastating little glimmer of gold in his eyes when he was amused, the sense of achievement she had once enjoyed when he laughed. No, she didn't, she absolutely didn't, she told herself with ferocious urgency. Which was just as well, she reminded herself. Luc might not have been exactly delighted to believe that the twins had been fathered by some other man, but he was likely to be even less happy when she told him the truth. It was going to be a very long and miserable summer, and tomorrow, when she informed Luc that he was a father, promised to be the very worst day of her life...

Star emerged from the bathroom and stopped dead, heart hammering so hard against her breastbone she felt faint, like someone in the grip of a severe anxiety attack. And no wonder! Luc had evidently made use of some other bathroom. Black hair still damp and gleaming, he was in the act of shedding a short silk robe. From across the room, Star watched the collar dipping, the light fabric drifting down to expose what had to be the most beautiful male back in the world. Smooth brown skin stretched taut over well-honed muscles. She shut her eyes tight in shame, denying herself

any more of a view. Averting her head, she scuttled over to
the bed to haul the spread from it.

'Goodnight,' she said in a tight little voice.

Luc climbed into bed, tossed back the duvet and threw
himself back against the pillows. Star was wearing an over-
size T-shirt with a large yellow duck motif back and front.
It wasn't remotely seductive. But his body seemed to think
otherwise and reacted with unquenchable enthusiasm. Star
bent down to arrange the spread on the sofa, revealing slender
legs to the top of her thighs, the cotton jersey of the T-shirt
stretching with provocative fidelity over the shapely curve of
her bottom...

His breath escaped in a soft hiss of reaction, the ache of
frustration becoming so powerful he clenched his long fingers. The anger still pent-up inside him began to smoulder
again. She was playing the tease deliberately. Star was no
longer the adoring little virgin he had, with commendable
adult restraint, contrived *not* to touch for the first six weeks
of their marriage.

'A little schoolgirl...' Gabrielle had composed her perfect
face into a pained grimace. 'Men who prey on schoolgirls
are *sick*, aren't they? But Star does ask for it. Those big
soppy puppy eyes of hers follow you about like you're a god
or something. How can you stand it?'

Surprisingly easily.

Snatched from that unwelcome recollection by the enervating sight of Star raising her arms high to comb her fingers
through her wet hair, Luc went rigid. The T-shirt pulled taut
over small breasts as firm and round as apples. Not free to
him *ever* again, Star had said. Smugly. The rage he had been
keeping a lid on for two and a half days surged higher still.
She was on the market and he would buy. Why not? He
would get her skinny, shameless little hide out of his system.
Long before the summer was over, he would be sated. No
woman had ever held him beyond a couple of months...and
one in a duck T-shirt had less hope than most.

Star could feel the silence buzzing around her like an electric storm. Goosebumps came out on her arms as she got into the makeshift bed, wishing Luc would switch out the lights. Then she could lie in the dark, hating herself without an audience. The dulled ache low in her stomach and the painful tightness of her sensitive breasts were a source of utter misery to her. She didn't trust herself to look back near him again, lest the craving get stoked to a level that he might notice. He noticed most things, did Luc. He missed nothing. He read her like a book when she could least afford to be read.

'*D'accord*...OK, now that you've given me the benefit of seeing what's on offer from every conceivable angle, I want the T-shirt off. And forget the sofa. I want you in this bed for the rest of the night,' Luc spelt out with crystal-clear clarity.

Totally disbelieving the evidence of her own ears, Star very slowly picked her head up and attempted to focus on Luc across the depth of the room. 'S-sorry?' she stammered helplessly.

Luc hauled himself off the pillows with one powerful hand. 'Don't you dare play games with me,' he warned in low-pitched but forceful continuance. 'I'm not in the mood for what you fondly imagine figures as verbal foreplay!'

Star sat up with a jerk, clutching the bedspread to herself. The pool of light round the vast bed illuminated the hard cast of his stunning dark features, the perceptible tension in the knotted muscles of his wide brown shoulders. The sheet was at his waist, startlingly white against his magnificent torso. He looked startlingly handsome and startlingly intimidating. Angry too. About what? She could feel that anger. Why was he so angry? What had she done?

'You seem to have the idea that I've been angling for some sort of approach,' Star breathed with hot cheeks, her annoyance with him somewhat tempered by the fear that she had somehow been putting out sexually inviting vibes as easily read as placards. 'But I honestly haven't been…at least, *not* knowingly.'

'You are as hungry for me as I am for you, *mon ange*,' Luc breathed in impatient interruption.

Star tore her dismayed eyes from his challenging scrutiny. 'You're very up-front about this sort of stuff, aren't you? Can I use an analogy here? If I ate as much chocolate as I'd like to, I wouldn't fit my clothes, so I control myself. Wanting to rip your clothes off all the time…well, it's much the same thing.'

'*Mon Dieu*…God give me strength,' Luc growled half under his breath.

'It *is*, whether you can see it or not,' Star persisted, pleating the spread between her restive, taut fingers and not looking at him lest she lose the thread of what she was trying to say. 'Last night we should just *leave* in the past—'

Luc groaned out loud.

'You're like too much chocolate, you're bad for me, and really don't want to be tempted to do what's bad for me…and bad for *you* too.'

Luc sprang out of bed. As he crossed the room, Star kept her head down and talked faster than ever. 'Now I could be really angry with you for phrasing your invitation to join you the way you did…but I'm making allowance for the fact that maybe you're annoyed with me for still seeming attractive to you. And maybe you're tired and just not used to having to *ask* with all these women throwing themselves at you…*what are you doing?*' she squealed in disconcertion.

Luc clamped his hands to her waist and lifted her off the sofa to hold her in mid-air. 'I am not bad for you. I am probably the sanest man you ever shared a bedroom with. Whether I'll still be sane at the end of the summer is anybody's guess. Think of me as a chocoholic, wholly at the mercy of ungovernable greed. Be compassionate,' he urged thickly.

Star remembered wanting him on his knees with lust for

her. Her own feet were dangling a good foot and a half off the floor. He wasn't quite begging but he was certainly on the road to very, very keen. And there was something in those stunning dark frustrated eyes that just filled her to overflowing with sympathy and longing and...?

As he interpreted the dreamy look in her aquamarine eyes with the instant recognition of a male who had once seen no other expression but that in her gaze, a blazing smile of satisfaction flashed across his lean strong face. Her heart literally tilted on its axis.

'Indulge yourself with me, *mon ange*,' Luc invited in a husky tone that made every nerve-ending in her treacherous body sit up and sing.

Common sense made a mighty and praiseworthy attempt to be heard inside her head. 'I can't...I *mustn't*!'

Luc laid her down on the bed with the sort of achingly tender care she had not experienced since his accidental consummation of their marriage. The thoughts in her head started seeming detached from reality.

Luc gazed down at her with glittering dark eyes of hunger and then stilled, a more grave expression forming on his darkly handsome features. 'Obviously I will look after you and the twins for as long as you need me to do so.'

'Look after me?' Reality was retreating so fast for Star that nothing short of a lightning strike was likely to bring it back. She was trembling, her pulses racing. The gloriously familiar scent of him was washing over her. After the emotional devastation which had followed their lovemaking the night before, there was now a sharper, needier, more desperate edge inside her; she had given him up and now he was back. She couldn't help but be caught up in a sense of how precious that was.

'*Naturellement*...I also believe that I can find you a house to live in here in France,' Luc mused with growling sensual huskiness, a whisper's breadth from her parted lips.

Her braincells surged together on the belief that something

enormously important was being said. Was he teasing her? A house in France? My goodness, how stupid she was being! Was he...could he be asking her to stay on at Chateau Fontaine? What *else* could he be doing? A tide of pure joy roared up through Star and left her feeling totally intoxicated. Her fingers slid into his luxuriant black hair and curved down to his magnificent cheekbones.

'House here in France?' she echoed like an obedient child, eager to encourage further revelations but scared of the big prize being withdrawn if she seemed too pushy or greedy or impatient.

'You'd like that...' Luc gathered, lowering his proud dark head to sensually taste her full lips.

Liked that, liked *everything*! The hunger he expressed with one kiss sent heat hurtling through her at storm-force potency. She kissed him back with all her heart and soul and let her palms rove with wondering delight over his powerful shoulders. Mine, mine, *mine*, she wanted to yell to the rooftops, but she also wanted to live out every fantasy of eighteen months away from him.

She pushed at his shoulders with as much force as she could muster, grateful enthusiasm leaping through her. She wanted to show him just how much she could learn if he would only give her the opportunity and the time to pick up more experience. Then he would never, ever think that he needed a mistress like Gabrielle Joly in his life again.

Luc fell back against the pillows, a slight hint of disconcertion in his intent dark gaze. 'What's wrong?'

'Nothing...absolutely nothing!' Star was just a little shy now, on the spot, as it were, with all those lights on while being aware that Luc was very much a sophisticate. She was absolutely terrified of doing something wrong and spoiling the moment. After all, sex had to be of crucial importance to Luc if just one night with her could persuade him to ask her to forget that theirs was supposed to be a fake reconciliation and make it a real one instead.

'Star...?' Luc curved a hand to her downbent head. 'I want you to be happy. I want to *make* you happy—'

'Oh...you're making me s-super-happy, because I—' Just adore you. She swallowed it back hastily, not wishing to show herself too keen too fast. Goodness knows, that hadn't got her very far before. Luc needed to believe that he had to make an effort to get those kind of results.

'You *need* someone like me.' Letting his fingers lace into her hair, Luc claimed a devouring kiss that left her quivering.

Intent on ensuring that he needed *her* even more, Star let an uncertain hand slide down over his taut stomach, fascinated by the way his muscles suddenly clenched and his equally sudden exhalation. She shifted position and bent her head, and let the tip of her tongue trace the intriguing little furrow of hair that ran down over his stomach and disappeared beneath the sheet. He jerked with satisfying responsiveness. Damp answering warmth surged at the very heart of her.

'*Later*...' His eyes blazing gold with desire, he tugged her up to him again, a ragged edge to his dark drawl. 'But now there's a couple of conditions to this arrangement that I need to be sure you understand and accept.'

Arrangement? In the act of drifting down to meet that wide sensual mouth like a programmed doll, Star found herself unexpectedly stayed by Luc's hands on her arms. 'Conditions?'

'I expect total fidelity from you for the duration.'

Her lashes fluttered over bewildered eyes. She was really fighting to concentrate now, because Luc was wearing that deadly serious look which always intimidated her into listening.

'Duration?' she repeated dutifully, rather like someone knowing only about five words of a foreign language but working hard to follow and comprehend.

'Inevitably this attraction will burn out.'

As Star stiffened, Luc locked both arms round her, brilliant megawatt eyes intent on her now troubled face. 'On the other hand, it could last for *ages*,' he extended, quick as a flash. 'But the other little condition I need to mention is that you'll have to be more discreet as my lover than you were as my wife. Emilie must *not* know.'

Star worked out the significance of that assurance very, very slowly, because her brain was functioning very, very slowly. And when it came to working out something that crucial to her life and her happiness, and she saw with stricken insight that nothing but sheer pain and disappointment awaited her, she didn't want to *think* any more.

But comprehension still marched on at supersonic speed. She had picked Luc up wrong. And wasn't that huge misapprehension as to his meaning entirely self-inflicted? She had been pathetically eager to believe that Luc was willing to give their marriage a real chance. But he had no intention of doing that. He *still* wanted a divorce.

Yet, in spite of that, he could ask her to stay on in France as his lover. *Lover?* A euphemism. Without love, she would just be his sexual partner, his mistress. Did he really think that she was that desperate to hold onto him? Enormous hurt enfolded Star like a blanket, chilling her overheated body to ice.

'Let go of me...' she said unsteadily.

'Yes...switch off that blasted phone of yours!' Luc agreed in exasperation, and willingly released her.

'Phone?' Star blinked, and only then did she hear the irritating buzz. She peered blankly at her bag, which was lying in a heap where she had left it earlier.

'I'll do it!' Luc offered.

'No...*no*!' Suddenly Star was flying off the bed and running to answer that phone as if her life depended on it.

In a sense it *did*. As the pain of renewed rejection settled on her, she just wanted to run and run from Luc. She snatched the mobile phone from her bag. Rory's voice greeted her. The tears came in reaction then, great, unstoppable rivulets pouring down her quivering cheeks. 'Rory…oh Rory!' she sobbed, and raced for the bedroom door to take the call in private.

CHAPTER SIX

STAR paced the floor of the giant front hall at Chateau Fontaine. 'I've got to be honest, Rory... I still care about Luc. I can't lie about that. All I've got to offer you is friendship, and you'd probably be better off without it while I'm feeling like this...'

'You're not short-changing me.' Rory's sigh carried down the phone line. 'You've never offered anything else; you've always held back.'

Still in the act of zipping up a pair of beige chinos, Luc reached the galleried landing above just as Star spoke again.

'I'm so grateful you're still speaking to me...you know, after everything I've just told you. I really, really love you for that!' Star admitted with tears stinging her eyes again.

'You married a really smooth rat—'

'I know he's a rat, but maybe that was the attraction,' Star muttered. 'I imagined I saw all sorts of other things, but now I see how stupid I was, and that has to be for the best, hasn't it?'

This was not eavesdropping, Luc told himself. He was in his own home listening to his wife telling her boyfriend she loved him. *Loved* him. The way she had loved *him* once? He wanted to yank the phone out of her hand and smash it to bits. Star was *his* wife! Wheeling round in his tracks, Luc strode away again, suddenly knowing only one thing for sure. He had no desire to hear any more.

But the strangest sensation of cold had begun spreading through Luc. He didn't like it. It was as if a big black cloud was rising at the back of his mind. In the space of little more than twenty-four hours, Star had got under his skin to the extent that he felt he wasn't in control any more. He liked that suspicion even less. But the inexplicable gap between what he was thinking and what he was actually doing could no longer be ignored. How else did he rationally explain asking Star to be his mistress? Where had that *insane* idea come from? Exactly when had a concept that far removed from reality crept into his subconscious mind?

It would be sheer madness. He wanted a divorce. He did not want to stay married to her. He didn't care if she loved another guy. He just wanted to kill the other guy...he just wanted to kill her. No, not her, *him*! That black cloud kept on rising; he couldn't concentrate. Perspiration beaded his skin. He clenched his fists in angry frustration. He didn't want to think. Suddenly, he understood that much. In the grip of the powerful nebulous feelings closing in on him, he felt alarmingly unstable. What he needed was a drink.

Star switched off the phone and sank down on one of the hall chairs. All she could think about was what an idiot she had been to imagine even briefly that Luc might want their marriage to continue. So he had asked her to be his mistress instead. Well, there was no prospect of her lowering herself to that level.

But then what other kind of offer could she have expected him to make? She *still* hadn't told Luc that he was the twins' father! Just when had she stopped remembering that? Why hadn't she paused to consider that letting Luc go on believing that Venus and Mars were another man's children was to fatally colour his view of her and change their relationship?

Oh, golly, gosh, what relationship? she asked herself painfully, her head in her hands as she sniffed. That winter, over eighteen months earlier, Luc had reunited her with Juno. Star and her mother had met first at Luc's Paris apartment. Afterwards, Luc had taken Star out to lunch. She hadn't realised then that there was already a woman in his life: Gabrielle Joly had been the ultimate in discretion.

'I think I fell in love with you the minute I saw you again,' she had announced over that lunch.

Luc dealt her an arrested glance.

'I didn't know anything could feel *this* intense,' she continued unsteadily. 'I suppose you're used to your looks knocking women flat, but what I notice most about you is how lonely you are—'

'I've never been lonely in my life,' Luc responded drily.

'I don't think you ever get close to anyone. I've been watching you. You freeze people out; you can't help yourself. Anything personal or emotional and you're really challenged to stay within a mile of the experience. Like now. You just want me to shut up and you want to escape without hurting my feelings,' she said guiltily. 'Well, thanks for listening to me. You can leave now if you like.'

He was trapped then for a little longer. She knew it, and had planned it that way, but her conscience twinged as she watched his long, beautifully shaped fingers close very tautly round his wine glass.

'You're just a child,' he began.

'No, I'm not a child. I seem like a child to you because I say things out loud that you wouldn't scream under the worst torture. I'm sorry, but this is the only way I had of getting through to you. You quite like being with me,' she pointed out shyly. 'Haven't you noticed that? And I notice you look at me, and then look away like you shouldn't be looking, and—'

'*Bon! Ca suffit maintenant.*' Rising from his seat, Luc glowered down at her from his impressive height. 'If you're not embarrassed for yourself, I am.'

'I know. But when you love someone as much as I love you—'

'You don't know what love is at your age,' he drawled with sudden lethal derision.

'I know more than you do. I don't think you've ever been in love in your whole life,' Star protested. 'Love's messy, and you're not. Love would make demands you wouldn't like and wouldn't want to spare the time for—'

Taking her by the arm when she knew that what he was really desperate to do was gag her into silence, Luc dragged her out of the exclusive restaurant, seemingly blind to the fascinated stares his unusual behaviour was attracting.

Out on the pavement, she whispered, 'I'm not expecting you to love me back, but doesn't it give you a warm feeling to know that someone loves you?'

Brilliant dark eyes hooded, Luc thrust her into the back seat of his limo. 'All that you're suffering from is adolescent hormones—'

'No, even if I could never, ever sleep with you, I would still *care* about you!' Star argued vehemently.

Luc studied her with even more glacial cool. Star got redder and redder, and eventually dropped her head. 'I'm sorry.' She hesitated, and then rushed on, 'Are you going to avoid me now? I couldn't *bear* that!'

'Of course I will not avoid you,' Luc rebutted in exasperation. 'But nor will we discuss this subject again. Is that understood?'

That same week, Luc had taken Emilie and Star to a dinner party held by some friends of his. Gabrielle Joly had been a guest as well, seated close to Luc and regularly engaging him in conversation. Gabrielle, with her endless legs, gorgeous blonde hair, exquisite face and svelte sophistication. Star felt so sick at the sight of what she feared might be the competition that she just couldn't eat.

'Tell me what you know about that Gabrielle woman,' Star urged Emilie later that evening.

Emilie reddened almost guiltily. 'I believe she was once a fashion model.' The older woman hesitated. 'I know no other way of putting this, Star...Gabrielle is Luc's mistress, and has been for quite some time.'

'His...*mistress*?' The bottom fell right out of Star's world.

'Don't look so horrified, Star. Frenchmen have always made convenient arrangements of that nature. Luc will never ask his mistress to play hostess at the chateau, but he'll so-

cialise freely with her everywhere else. Gabrielle would've
been invited for his benefit this evening. She uses a house
just a few miles from here.'

Pale as death, hearing the hollow note in Emilie's recita-
tion, Star produced a ragged laugh. 'I wish you'd mentioned
her existence sooner, Emilie.'

'I didn't want to put you off Luc,' Emilie admitted ruefully. 'Whether he realises it or not, he's already very much
attracted to you. Your warmth draws him like a magnet.
When he walks into a room, you're the first person he looks
for, and if you're not there he can't settle until he knows
where you are.'

'But he already has *her*—'

'Oh, well, if you can't accept that a man of almost thirty
comes with some worldly experience, you'd be wise to give
up on him. And that would be a shame. We all need to be
loved. If he doesn't meet the right girl soon, the kind of girl
who's not afraid to fight through those barriers of his, he's
likely to end up as unhappy as his poor father is now.'

Was it any wonder that with such constant eager encouragement Star continued to love Luc to distraction? And
Emilie might have known how Star felt about Luc, but Star
didn't confide in her mother, who was by then renting an
apartment in Nantes. Determined to have nothing to do with
the Sarrazins, Juno refused to visit Star at the chateau. For
her daughter to love Luc Sarrazin would have seemed the
ultimate disloyalty. So Star kept quiet.

But then fate took a hand: Roland Sarrazin had a heart
attack and was rushed into hospital with Emilie by his side.
In all the fuss, Star forgot that she should have visited her
mother that day. That evening, Luc returned from the hospital, looking exhausted. Star rushed to offer sympathy.

'Do you want to talk about how you feel?' she asked.

'No.'

'Do you want me to talk about something else?'

'No.'

Luc nodded grim agreement.

'But you *can't* want to be on your own!' Closing her hand over his sleeve to prevent him from moving away, as he always did when she got too close, Star looked up at him with pleading eyes. 'Isn't there *anything* I can do to make you feel better?'

Glittering dark eyes gazed down into hers. *'Go—'*

'Luc, *please—'*

And then he just grabbed her, literally grabbed her up into his arms and brought his mouth down hot and hard and hungry on hers. The shock of that sudden onslaught knocked Star sideways, but his explosive passion blazed up through her like a bush fire. She couldn't get enough of him and clung like superglue. When Juno was shown into Luc's library by the housekeeper, Star was welded to every available inch of Luc in enraptured surrender.

There was the most awful scene, with her mother hurling all sorts of ridiculous accusations and threatening to go to the newspapers. After Juno stormed out again, Luc, who had uttered not a single word in his own defence, turned to Star, where she was cringing with shamefaced guilt. 'We'll have to move fast to spike your mother's guns.'

'She didn't *mean* those things she said!'

'She's very bitter, and right now my father's peace of mind is of paramount importance. A sordid scandal would destroy him. Since I invited this situation, I must ensure that there are no repercussions,' Luc drawled flatly, no emotion of any kind showing in his lean strong face. 'The only way I can do that is to marry you as quickly as possible. Your mother can get no immoral mileage out of that development.'

'M-marry me? You're asking—?'

'Not a *real* marriage,' Luc emphasised drily. 'When the need for a cover story is past, we'll get an annulment. So don't get excited, *mon ange*. Nothing has changed.'

Star clasped her trembling hands together. 'Do I get a wedding ring?'

Luc gave a grudging nod.

'A dress?'

'No.'

'What's wrong with me *pretending* it's a proper wedding?'

'Your imagination doesn't need encouragement.'

They married in a civil ceremony in Nantes, attended only by Emilie and Luc's lawyer. It was not a secret marriage, but neither was it publicised, and, with Roland Sarrazin so ill, people might have questioned their timing, but not the quietness of the ceremony.

Her father-in-law asked to see her after the wedding he had been too weak to attend.

'I would not dream of questioning Luc's choice of bride,' the older man sighed, surprising Star with that assurance while simultaneously appraising her with a morose dissatisfaction that ensured she would not get a swollen head. 'I hope I know better than to interfere in my son's private life.'

Before Star's thoughts could stray on to the devastating disillusioning reality of having been abandoned on her wedding night for another woman, the cold marble beneath her bare feet became uncomfortable enough to dredge her out of her memories. But she still found herself recalling when, later, a minor car smash had put Luc into Casualty with concussion and sent her running panic-stricken to his side. Flatly refusing to be hospitalised overnight, Luc had come home with her. She had just adored fussing round him, insisting he go to bed and getting her crystals out, determined to heal his headache away.

Now she shied away from the recollection of how appallingly immature she had been just eighteen months earlier, and stood up in sudden decision. It might be the middle of the night, but it was time she came clean with Luc about their children at least. Maintaining that fiction was unfair to him.

But when Star returned to the bedroom, Luc was nowhere to be seen. Too worked up now to settle again, Star pulled

on jeans and a top and went off to find him. Her troubled
reflections marched on. How did she stop craving what Luc
could never give? A man couldn't be forced into loving. So
why did she keep on letting her emotions get the better of
her? Why had she kidded herself that she was strong enough
to spend one last night with Luc? That one night had plunged
her back into emotional turmoil. That one night had convinced Luc that she would quite happily settle for sex if she
could have him no other way. And Luc, ever the banker, was
programmed to take advantage of the best deal he could get.
Instead of crying like a drippy wimp, she should have lifted
one of those giant ornate lamps in the bedroom and simply
brained him with it!

Star had worked up quite a temper by the time she saw
the light burning under the door of the library on the ground
floor and walked in.

Luc was by the window, a brandy goblet clasped in one
lean hand. His hair-roughened chest and his feet were bare,
a dark green shirt hanging open over his well-cut chinos.
Dressed so casually, and with his jawline darkened by stub-
ble, he looked incredibly unfamiliar to her disconcerted appraisal.

'Go back to bed,' Luc advised flatly.

Even though he was standing in the shadows cast by the
desk lamp, Star recognised his seething tension and came to
a halt several feet away, scanning the fierce angularity of his
dark golden features, the warning flash in his eyes before he
veiled them and the rigidity of his broad shoulders.

'Just for once, do as I ask!' Luc raked with sudden unconcealed fury.

Startled into taking a backward step, Star studied him in
honest bewilderment. 'What have *you* got to be so angry
about? I certainly didn't ask for this situation with Emilie to
develop.'

'My anger dates back a lot further than yesterday. There

was no ''situation'' until you decided that you were in love with me and refused to back off.'

Her natural colour receded under that surprise attack. 'But—'

'Before I married you, I saw only your youth and vulnerability. I didn't appreciate how far you would go to get what you want!' Eyes burnished gold with anger sought out and held hers. 'The first time you approached me I should have squashed you beyond all hope of recovery! But I was reluctant to hurt you. You *played* on that—'

'No…' Star made a tiny awkward movement of appeal with her hand. 'Not deliberately—'

'I thought you were sweet, essentially harmless…' A roughened laugh was wrenched from Luc. 'But from the minute you came into my life you've been as destructive as an enemy tank!'

Star was paralysed to the spot by the shattering effect of Luc casting aside his reserve and getting truly personal. The anger and bitterness he was revealing really shook her up.

'I'm drunk…' Luc breathed grimly, as if she had asked a question.

Luc drunk? That struck Star as so extraordinary she just gaped at him. He didn't look drunk, but he certainly wasn't behaving with his usual chilling self-command. He had compared her to an enemy tank. She tried to force a smile at that colourful image, but she couldn't. Shock went on spreading through her, and beneath it only guilt was rising in strength.

'A lot of men would have taken you up on your invitation that winter.' Shimmering dark eyes welded to her in unconcealed condemnation. 'You were very sexy. I was never unaware of your attraction. I was never indifferent, but I kept my distance.'

'Luc, I didn't kn—'

'I went against my father's wishes when I reunited you with your mother. And *how* was I rewarded?'

At that unwelcome question, Star's tummy just flipped.

'One lousy kiss and I end up having to get married,' Luc framed jaggedly, pale with sheer outrage at that recollection. 'But that wasn't the end of it, was it? You *still* wouldn't take no for an answer.'

'Please don't say any more, Luc…' Star urged in desperation. 'If I could go back and change things, I would, but I can't! I was obsessed with you…and I'm sorry…but I couldn't help that, nor could I see how selfish I was being.'

'You waited until I had a concussion,' Luc continued between gritted white teeth, his husky accent fracturing audibly. 'Then you slunk into bed with me when I was asleep. How *low* can a woman sink?'

Star studied the rug and watched it blur under her filling eyes. Seen through *his* eyes, framed in *his* words, her behaviour seemed even worse in retrospect. Yet after that night she had judged herself equally harshly. That was why she had left France. She hadn't run away; she had simply seen that the very least she could do was get out of Luc's life and leave him in peace.

Momentarily, she was tempted to mention the role which Gabrielle Joly had played in that final decision. But now that Gabrielle was gone from Luc's life Star was too proud and still too sensitive on that subject to admit how disillusioned and hurt she had been by the other woman's apparent hold on Luc. In those days, their marriage had been very much a fake, she reminded herself.

'And when I finally dared to tell you that no woman was going to trap me into a marriage I didn't want with sex, what did you do?' Luc's dark deep drawl had dropped to a seething whisper of what sounded like near uncontrollable rage.

'The only thing I could do. I went away,' she answered heavily.

At that response, Luc shuddered. 'You went away,' he echoed unsteadily. 'You did *not* just go away!'

In bewilderment, Star stared at him. 'What are you getting at?'

'You left me a letter telling me you couldn't *live* without me and vanished into thin air!' Luc shot at her in savage condemnation, devastating her with the force of his anger.

'What was wrong with that?'

'*What was wrong with that?*' Luc practically whispered his incredulity at that response, black fury emanating from him in blistering waves. 'I thought you'd gone off to drown yourself! I had the moat dragged...I put frogmen in the bloody lake!'

She regarded him as if he had taken leave of his wits.

'If you laugh...if you *laugh*...' Luc warned her thickly.

But Star was already picturing the extreme anxiety it would have taken to persuade Luc to embark on such a search. Her stomach turned over sickly. There was no risk of her being amused.

'Not once did it occur to you that I might be concerned for your welfare. Not once in all those months we were apart did you even phone to tell me that you were *all right*!' Swinging away from her, Luc sent the goblet in his hand flying into the fireplace, where it exploded noisily into crystal fragments.

Star studied those gleaming fragments in deep, deep shock. 'I...I didn't think—'

'You don't *ever*. You live every day like it's going to be your last. You don't look back, you don't look forward, you just do what you *feel* like. That's a luxury some of us have never known,' Luc stated glacially, his anger clearly spent.

Trembling in the face of all those sins he had piled up into a giant weight with which to crush her, Star was parchment-pale. Irresponsible, selfish, flighty. It seemed she had no redeeming graces. She was guilty as hell, she conceded wretchedly. She had thrown herself at him. She had also allowed him to marry her when she should have confronted her mother and at least tried to persuade her into withdrawing her unjust threats. During their brief time together after their marriage, she had refused to accept rejection. But, surprisingly, it appeared that in Luc's eyes her biggest sin had been vanishing and failing to contact him in all the months that had followed.

'You even persuaded Emilie to pretend that she didn't know where you were all that time,' Luc concluded grimly. 'Do you think I didn't realise that today? Emilie who might have been my mother, had my father had the courage to stand by her!'

Her utter confusion at that allusion made him release a weary laugh.

'You see nothing but what relates directly to you.' Luc shook his proud dark head in despair. 'Why do you think it was so important for Emilie to be there for my father when he was dying? Why do you think her presence was such a comfort? When they were young, they were in love. But my grandfather disapproved because Emilie was a poor relation. My father was afraid of losing out to his younger brother in the inheritance stakes and he gave Emilie up. She went on to make a happy marriage; *he* didn't.'

Listening to Luc spell out what she felt she should have sensed or worked out for herself made Star feel even worse. It was like the missing piece in a puzzle, which she had been too self-absorbed to recognise as a puzzle... Emilie's constant attendance on Roland Sarrazin that winter, her quiet, but undeniably deep grief when he finally passed away.

'Emilie felt sorry for him, desperately sorry for him, because he never stopped caring for her. After my mother died, my father would have married Emilie, but she turned him down.'

'You're right...' Star mumbled ruefully. 'I don't see anything that's not directly under my nose. I thought I was so perceptive too.'

'Go to bed...it's three in the morning.'

Star still hadn't told him about Venus and Mars. Now the prospect of making that announcement loomed over her like a death sentence. If he didn't hate her yet, he could only be a hair's breadth from doing so. She saw that in so many ways Luc had been amazingly tolerant of her behaviour. And she didn't think tolerance came naturally to him. Indeed, with his legendary reputation for cold rationality and ruthlessness, all of a sudden it was very hard to grasp *why* Luc had allowed one foolish teenager to cause him so much grief…

'Just one more thing…' Luc remarked flatly, breaking into her thoughts. 'What I said about buying a house here for you? It was a foolish impulse, and I apologise for making the suggestion.'

'Maybe you wanted revenge…' Star suddenly felt as if she had been smacked in the face with the ultimate of rejections. His apology was undeniably sincere. Evidently one good long look at the catastrophic results of having her in his life had cured Luc of the smallest desire to continue their relationship in any form. And she really didn't feel that she could blame him, which felt even worse.

'I don't think like that…'

Luc watched Star sidling backwards out of the room with a kind of blind look in her eyes and wondered why he didn't feel better. He wondered why he suddenly felt like the sort of male who was brutal to small children and animals. He wondered why, when it was natural for him to be extremely tough on those who surrounded him, being tough on Star had demanded the spur of eighteen months of pent-up rage finally breaking its boundaries. But sanity had reasserted its natural sway, he told himself in grim consolation, wincing as Star bashed one slight shoulder on the corner of the bookshelves before finally disappearing from view.

He was amazed that she hadn't shouted back at him. Strange how dissatisfying an experience that had proved. But then alcohol was a depressant; he had lost his temper and he loathed being out of control. Possibly he had been a little too tough on her. But revenge? Trust Star to come up with that angle! He was *above* that sort of nonsense.

Upstairs, Star collapsed down on the bedroom sofa without

even taking off her clothes. Her life seemed to stretch before her like a desert of grey desolation. Luc just about hated her and had no reason whatsoever to think well of her. Yet she did find herself questioning why Luc had held onto his anger for so long. Flattened by exhaustion, however, she slept for four hours, and woke up feeling unrefreshed.

Luc's bed was empty, untouched from the night before. It was seven. She headed straight into the bathroom, peeling off clothing as she went. After a frantically quick wash, she donned the black sand-washed silk hooded summer dress which her mother had given her for her birthday. It felt suitably funereal.

With the twins' birth certificates clutched in one nerveless hand, she went straight downstairs. Her steps getting slower and slower, she entered the imposing dining room. Luc was seated in aristocratic isolation at the far end of the polished table. He lowered his newspaper, revealing hooded eyes and a grim cast to his dark good-looks. Immaculate in a silver-grey suit worn with a silk shirt and a burgundy silk tie, he looked formidable, but he still stopped her susceptible heart clean dead in its tracks.

'I didn't expect to see you up this early,' he admitted with complete cool.

'I…I needed to speak to you before you left for the bank.' Star sucked in a deep, deep breath and forced herself to walk down the length of the table towards him.

Luc folded his newspaper and rose with lithe grace. 'I'm afraid you left it too late. I'm about to leave.'

'Luc…these are the twins' birth certificates,' she practically whispered, pale as milk.

'Of what possible interest could they be to me?' Luc didn't pause even to spare the documents a glance as he strode down the other side of the table in the direction of the door.

Star turned again, her rigid backbone tightening another painful notch. 'The twins were born *more* than six months ago, Luc. They're twelve months old...they just don't look it because they were premature—'

Luc swung back with a frown of complete exasperation. 'Why are you unloading all this stuff on me?'

'Venus and Mars are twelve months old, you see,' Star continued in a fast fading voice. 'That night...you know, when I "slunk", as you put it, you-know-where...well, that night had consequences. I'm really sorry.'

CHAPTER SEVEN

Luc studied Star, absently noting that she was wearing a nightie that resembled some sort of mourning apparel and that she lacked her usual glow.

His brain had shrieked to a sudden halt on her second reference to the age of her children. Twelve months...*twelve months old*? What were they? Miniature babies? What was she trying to tell him? Premature? Born too early, he rephrased for his own benefit. Was there something wrong with the twins? Were they ill? A momentary image of those helpless little creatures under threat gripping him, Luc paled as if a spooky hand had trailed down his spine.

'They're your kids,' Star framed unevenly. 'I should have put you right the minute I realised you thought otherwise. But I was shocked, and annoyed that you could think that they were some other man's. Since you didn't seem that bothered by the idea, I didn't contradict you.'

'*My* kids...' Luc echoed in the unreacting manner of a male who had not yet computed what he was being told. 'What's the matter with them? Are they sick?'

Now it was Star's turn to look confused. 'No, of course not. They're fine now, and catching up great. Luc...do you understand what I've just told you?'

'You said they were my children,' Luc repeated back to her, still without any change of expression, although his winged ebony brows were beginning to pleat.

'I really don't know where you got the idea that they *weren't*—'

'Emilie's accountant said the twins had only got out of hospital in the autumn. He assumed that they were newborns

103

then…*certainement.*' His usual level diction rose in volume, a dark frown slowly building.

For Star, who was feeling nauseous with nerves, that silence was unbearable.

'*J'etais vraiment fâché…*' Luc murmured in fluid French.

I was angry as hell, Star translated, watching Luc, bracing herself for a sudden massive explosion, every muscle in her slender length straining taut. Without warning, he moved again, and she jerked, only to look on in utter bewilderment as he headed towards the housekeeper, who was standing about thirty yards away in the hall, positioned by the front door in readiness for his punctual exit.

Luc was engaged in recalling the way Star had used to see him off every morning, no matter how early the hour of his departure, no matter how discouraging his mood. Chitchat at breakfast wasn't his style. Star had been impervious to the message of his silence. She had torn up his croissant for him in the most infuriatingly invasive and messy manner, poured his coffee, and talked and talked with endless sunny good cheer, deflated not one jot by his monosyllabic replies.

She had been waiting for him when he'd come home as well, surging across the bridge to greet him, always hurling herself at him as if he had been away for at least a month. It had never mattered who was with him either. A party of important diplomats or high-ranking bankers, he mused, all of them had been instantly fascinated by her quicksilver energy, her innate charm, her incredible legs…

Now he was undoubtedly confronting a future of having his croissant mangled… *Ah, c'est la vie,* Luc conceded with a sigh. Congratulating himself on his self-control, not to mention his remarkable cool in crisis, he informed his housekeeper that he would not be flying to Paris after all. He then strolled out into the fresh air, where he breathed in slow and deep to counteract the infuriating light-headed sensation assailing him.

Had he considered himself to be an emotional individual,

he might have wondered if what he was experiencing was shock combined with the most intense relief. But a complete stranger to all such self-analysis, and a male who reasoned solely in practical terms of cause and effect, Luc decided that he was suffering for his alcoholic indulgence several hours earlier.

Striding in the direction of the heli-pad, he was even more happily engaged in rationally reviewing obvious facts which might not immediately appear as obvious to Star as they were to him. Point one, he thought, smiling at the prospect, Rory would now sadly be nothing more for Star than a fleeting thought of what might have been, but was *not* to be. All children deserved two caring parents living under the same roof.

Frozen in position by one of the tall dining-room windows, Star watched Luc approach the waiting helicopter with eyes of complete incomprehension. He spoke to his pilot, sunlight glinting off his luxuriant black hair, one lean hand thrust with casual nonchalance in the pocket of his well-cut trousers. Star could not credit what she was seeing. He looked so relaxed, not at all like a male who had just been given a revelation of earth-shaking magnitude. Maybe he had walked outdoors in an effort to keep a tight rein on his temper. Maybe *she* just couldn't read body language. When had she ever known what was happening inside that tortuously complex brain of his?

Striding back through the front door, emitting a strong air of decisiveness, Luc headed straight for the stairs. Star hurried across the hall in his wake. 'Where are you going?'

'To see my children.'

The sound of the possessive pronoun he used off-balanced Star.

Bertille had already fed and dressed the twins, and as soon as she saw their parents appear, she smiled and slipped out. Luc stilled in the centre of the room, just staring at the two babies playing on the carpet, his bold profile taut.

Venus cried, 'Mum-mum!' and began to crawl towards Star.

'They can move independently…and *talk*?' Luc breathed in almost comical amazement.

'Well, Venus knows two words…those two.' Star was watching Mars. Her son could only crawl backwards. Brought to a halt by the barrier of the wall, he loosed a plaintive wail, big brown eyes filling with tears of frustration.

As Star went to help, Luc startled her by getting there first. Hunkering down with athletic ease, he lifted Mars and spoke to him in husky French. A total pushover for all affection and attention, Mars's tears dried up like magic. Beaming, he snuggled into the shelter of Luc's arm with the air of a baby who would be quite happy to spend the rest of the day there.

'He's so trusting…' Luc commented in a roughened aside, torn between the child he held and Venus, who, intrigued by his presence, had switched direction from her mother to make a beeline for him instead.

Planting herself back on her bottom, Venus tugged at the tassel on one of Luc's shoes. Then she threw her bright curly head back and looked up at him with a playful smile of challenge.

Luc extended his free hand in welcome. Venus gripped his thumb. Then she let go to make a frantic grab at the gold watch she had just noticed gleaming on his wrist. At that sudden switch of focus, Luc's rare smile broke out, amusement lighting up his lean strong face. 'She's like a miniature clone of her mother.'

Her heart rocked by that intensely charismatic smile, Star's mouth ran dry. 'Well, Mars takes after you.'

In fact it was as if their respective genes had known better than to try to mix in their offspring, Star reflected ruefully. Mars got upset if his routine was disrupted, and when he played his ability to concentrate was already noticeable. Venus did everything at high speed and took life just as it came.

As the minutes passed, with Luc wholly engaged on interaction with the twins, Star's tension steadily increased. She just couldn't believe what she was seeing. Careless of his beautiful expensive suit, Luc was now seated on the carpet with Venus and Mars swarming over him as if he was a large and novel toy. Little hands were snatching at his tie, digging into his pockets, pulling at his hair and exploring his face.

Star had never dreamt that Luc might drop his dignified reserve to allow all that close bodily contact and over-familiarity. In fact she would have sworn that he would run a mile from such treatment. Nor had she appreciated that learning that the twins were his might enable Luc to relax and handle their children with much greater confidence than he had shown before.

Indeed, the most awful biting jealousy surged up through Star as she stood there. She was totally ignored by all. She had even been denied her usual enthusiastic early-morning welcome from her babies. And she was now an unwilling audience to the birth of what appeared to be a mutual admiration society for three.

'They're both yawning,' Luc commented a whole twenty-five minutes later, his disappointment audible.

'You've overtired them,' Star heard herself snipe, although she was well aware that after their disturbed night the day before both children would have a much greater need for a long morning nap.

Star settled the twins back into their cots, but not before quite a few hugs and kisses had been exchanged.

'I didn't expect such young children to accept me so easily,' Luc finally drawled, finding himself as ignored as Star had felt ten minutes earlier.

Star turned her head, shining copper hair framing the tight expression on her triangular face. 'They're very fond of Rory, and because of him they like and trust all men,' she said dismissively.

Luc gazed steadily back at her, stunning dark eyes un-

readable as an overcast night sky, but his magnificent bone
structure was taut beneath his smooth golden skin.

'So can I expect to see a lot of you in England after the
end of the summer?' Star asked brittly. 'You know, I'm
homesick already.'

'We'll discuss that downstairs,' Luc informed her, and
strode out.

I just bet we will, Star thought, resenting the way Luc
automatically assumed charge and closing out the little voice
that warned that she was being mean and nasty. After all,
just at that minute she felt like being *horribly* mean and
nasty. It felt better than dwelling on the physical ache of
painful yearning which Luc could rouse in her just by being
in the same room. She could even justify nastiness as a necessary defense mechanism against a male who had hurt her
as much as Luc had hurt her during the early hours of the
morning...

First wanting her, then rejecting her, but not before he had
picked out every one of her failings and held them up to her,
so that she could know what an awful person she was. That
seemed to be a pattern with Luc too. It was as if every time
he felt he might be getting too close to her he just instantly
switched off again and dragged up every reason under the
sun to keep his distance.

And what she had said about Rory *was* true...up to a point,
she reasoned. Rory was fond of the twins, but he really saw
them as an extension of Star, while Luc had instinctively
responded to their son and daughter as individuals and had
awarded them and *not* Star his full attention. Was that a sin
or a virtue? she asked herself bitterly.

Coffee had been laid out in the main salon when Star finally came downstairs again. While he'd entertained Venus
and Mars, Luc had appeared more relaxed than she had ever
seen him. Now she absorbed his cool and distant expression
and veiled eyes. In a split second her nervous tension mushroomed. So Luc had accepted the existence of his children

and had spent some time with them, but that certainly didn't mean he was *pleased* that the wife he was planning to divorce had made him a father.

And if Luc was about to throw recriminations, Star wanted them over with as soon as possible. 'Well?' she said baldly, giving him the opening.

'Coffee?' Luc proffered smoothly.

'Coffee makes me sick when I'm nervous!'

Luc poured himself a cup with the kind of cool that set her teeth on edge.

'Well?' she prompted a second time. 'Just go on. *Say* it!'

Luc raised a politely enquiring brow. 'What is it you wish me to say?'

In a whirl of sand-washed silk and frustration, Star spun away again, bangles jangling on her slender wrist in tinkling accompaniment. 'If I hadn't sneaked into bed with you, you wouldn't be a father now!'

'I knew what I was doing, *mon ange*.'

Star whirled round again, aquamarine eyes confused.

'Did you notice me struggling?' Luc enquired drily.

Her cheeks warmed.

'Naturally not,' Luc answered for himself. 'I was enjoying myself far too much to call a halt, and I didn't protect you from pregnancy. The responsibility for the conception of our children is undoubtedly *all* mine.'

His absolute self-command disconcerted Star just as much as what he was saying. After all, the enemy tank he had likened her to had taken surprise hostages. And possibly Luc was still in shock at that development.

'You don't have to take the blame,' she began, sounding more like her usually fair self. 'I knew—'

'You knew *nothing*,' Luc stressed with a wry twist of his sensual mouth. 'Isn't that the definitive point?'

Her face burned at that incontrovertible fact. She might have known about the birds and the bees the night the twins had been conceived, but the combination of boarding school and Emilie's careful supervision had given Star little opportunity to experiment. A few over-enthusiastic clinches with teenage boys had not prepared her for the distinct but delicious shock of sharing a bed with a fully grown adult male possessed of the ability to give her the ultimate in pleasure.

Luc moved to lift the birth certificates which she had last seen in the dining room from the magnificent mantelpiece. Although only he could have been responsible for having moved them, he perused the certificates afresh with a decided hint of fascination. 'Viviene and Maximilian...Viviene and Max Sarrazin,' he sounded out softly.

'*Known* as Venus and Mars,' Star stressed, pausing in her restive movements round the room.

'But my son and my daughter, who will naturally be brought up here in their family home.' Luc was very still, the long, lean flow of his powerful body perfectly poised by the superb fireplace.

Taken aback by that confident statement, Star dropped dead and stared. 'What are you talking about?'

His brilliant dark eyes were steady as a rock in his lean strong face. 'I think you should sit down and have some coffee. All this frantic pacing up and down must be making you dizzy—'

'Look, I'm not dizzy!' Star folded her arms tight. 'I don't want to sit down either.'

'And I don't want to argue with you, but if you force the issue, you'll find yourself on a losing streak,' Luc warned.

Her eyes fired with quick resentful anger. 'Will I indeed? Five minutes after finding out you're a father, you start making outrageous statements and trying to lay down the law.'

'And I should add that the law—French family law, at least—will come down on my side,' Luc drawled with cool exactitude.

Goosebumps rising on her bare arms, Star went rigid. 'What are you trying to say?'

'That a description of the home environment in which you

were keeping my children in England would be very much
in my favour in a French court.'

Star turned pale. 'You're threatening me…'

'You're shocked,' Luc noted. 'Why? Sadly, the twins are
more entitled to tender treatment right now than you are, *mon
ange.*'

'You *are* threatening me…' Shaken disbelief was splin-
tering through Star.

'You should know where you stand. Between a rock and
a hard place,' Luc told her helpfully, lest she be too slow to
have absorbed that message. 'No way are you removing my
children from beneath this roof at the end of the summer and
taking them back to England with you!'

'You *can't*—'

'I *can* stop you. I would dislike the means I would have
to utilise, but I would do it,' Luc countered levelly. 'You've
made some unwise decisions since our children were born—'

'Like what?' Star slammed back at him ungrammatically,
thrown into a greater panic by every word he voiced with
such intimidating calm.

'In spite of the fact that you were existing below the poverty line, you didn't inform me of their birth nor did you ask
for my financial support. Now even *I* am aware of the accepted authority which states that the needs of the child
should always come first.' Luc sent her a winging glance of
reproof. 'In attempting to raise our children in an undesirable
environment, while also denying me my rights as a father,
you failed to behave like a mature and responsible parent.'

Star's soft lips fell open in appalled incredulity at that
judgement.

Luc screened his penetrating gaze and spread his lean
hands in a wry, dismissive gesture. 'Now, I don't believe it
would be fair to judge the teenager you were at the time of
their birth against that particular yardstick. But you must accept that in any custody dispute you will be compared to me,

and my worst enemy couldn't label me as either immature or irresponsible.'

It was a terrifyingly impressive conclusion. By the time Luc had finished speaking, he had succeeded in seriously scaring Star. A custody dispute in which what she could offer their children would be measured against what Luc could offer? Luc, with several centuries of solid family respectability behind him and every one of his gloomy ancestors born in wedlock. Luc, with his immense wealth and with his opinions on global financial problems sought by the highest placed politicians in Europe. Star's blood simply ran cold.

'I just don't understand any of this...' Star was fighting to keep a grip on her turbulent emotions. 'The instant you find out that the twins are yours, you immediately start threatening to take them from me—'

'No, that's not either my wish or my intention. But, ironically, it is exactly what you did to me before I came downstairs again,' Luc drawled very quietly. 'Were you expecting me to jump for joy when you announced that you were already homesick and you talked about returning to England?'

Star reddened and looked away with extreme awkwardness. 'No...but—well, OK, maybe it was a threat,' she muttered in an undertone.

'Thank you. But although you've finally told me that the twins are my children, you don't appear to have the slightest grasp of how much that fact is going to impact on *all* our lives.'

'But why should it change anything?' Star demanded. 'I'm quite happy for you to see them as much as you want—'

'Will you please explain to me why you can't accept that I should want my own children as much as you want them?' Luc enquired, with what appeared to be sincere incomprehension.

Her bewilderment and fear flipped into total panic at that announcement. 'Because you didn't want *me*, didn't want to be *married*, for goodness' sake!' Star practically shrieked back at him. 'Why would I ever think that you would welcome being saddled with two kids from that same stupid *fake* marriage? I thought you'd be furious if you found out I was pregnant! I thought you'd want me to have a termination! I thought you'd be outraged with me for creating such an ongoing problem…'

'So you made some very wild assumptions and created a really huge ongoing problem. That doesn't make any kind of sense to me,' Luc admitted with the strangest half-smile of evident acceptance. 'But then not a lot of what you do makes sense to me, so it doesn't matter. What *does* matter is that you're becoming very upset.'

Star gulped back the thickness of tears in her throat. 'And you're surprised?'

Luc took a slow, fluid step closer. 'How can I be a father to two children living in a different country? I can't agree to that. Perhaps I came on too hot and heavy, but you have ties back in England that I want you to put behind you now.'

Star blinked, her breath snarling up in her throat. Ties? *What* ties? What had she to put behind her? Four hours of sleep had left her brain less than agile, but Luc appeared to be firing on all four cylinders, like a Ferrari ready to roar down a race track.

'I'm referring to Rory,' Luc clarified without hesitation. 'I won't stand back and allow a casual lover to take *my* place with my children.'

She almost told him that she had never slept with Rory, but then angry defensiveness and pride overcame the desire to be that honest. What business was it of his? How many women had he slept with since she had last been in France? Gabrielle might be old history but that didn't mean that Luc had become celibate. And what right did a male set on divorcing her have to dictate what she did in her own life? The *right* of power and influence, her intelligence warned her at that point. Luc had already said that if she tried to take the twins home he would go to court and, at the very least, prevent her from removing them from France.

Star jerked in even greater confusion as Luc suddenly reached for her fiercely clenched hands to draw her to him.

'What are you doing?' she gasped.

'Once you told me that the only thing in the world you would *ever* want was to be my wife, and that if you couldn't have me your life wouldn't be a life any more...it would just be an existence, shorn of all sunlight and happiness, because inside yourself you would just want to die,' Luc recited in his rich, dark accented drawl.

Star just froze. The words were vaguely recognisable. Her note, her goodbye note eighteen months earlier! Her lashes fluttered and then stayed deliberately down low, because at that precise moment she could not have looked Luc in the face to save her life. The cringe factor of that cruelly sharp memory of his was high, indeed sufficient to make her entire bodily surface blush.

'And you wonder *why* I had the moat dragged...' Luc murmured gently. 'But now I'm asking you to put your money where your mouth is.'

Star blinked. 'P-put my money where my m-mouth is?' she stammered helplessly.

'Yes, and live up to all those heartfelt sentiments...*ah, non,*' Luc scolded softly as she suddenly attempted to wrench free of his determined hold.

'You're trying to send me up!' she condemned hotly.

'No. For the sake of our children, I'm challenging you to forget Rory and concentrate your attention back on me and our marriage,' Luc contradicted tautly. 'I accept that that will *be* a challenge for you. But I'm hoping that even if you can't recover that original enthusiasm, some day you could be happy with me again.'

For the sake of our children? Concentrate on our marriage? Those were the only two phrases which Star absorbed from that speech. All the rest of what he said might as well have been directed at a brick wall. A heady mix of anguished pain and humiliation engulfed her like a drowning tidal wave. So that was what he was after now! Total possession of Venus and Mars, with her as a useful adjunct on the home front. Violent hurt shuddered through Star. All of a sudden Luc didn't want a divorce any more. But *she* herself had played no part in his change of heart! What she had wanted and prayed for through eighteen endless months he was ready to give after spending only half an hour with their children! That was an unbelievable cruelty.

'Are you cold?' Luc demanded anxiously. 'Why are you shaking?'

'You insensitive toad!' Star hurled rawly, her head flying up, aquamarine eyes blazing with outraged pain as she jerked free of him and stalked towards the door. 'How dare you ask that of me after all you've put me through? You know, you may be the cat's whiskers of a brain at the bank, but I don't think you know diddly-squat about anything else in life!'

Luc reached the door first and slammed it fast, while he attempted to identify what he had said wrong. He had worked out that speech while he was playing with the twins, satisfied that it covered every potential rock on which he might run aground. He could have told her he thought she was like a butterfly, lighting on whichever male was within closest reach at any given time. He could have told her that her great love for Rory would enjoy as much longevity as her love for himself evidently had. And that when it came to loyalty in love she was horrendously unstable, and that for as long as *he* was her husband, he wouldn't be trusting her out of his sight. But he had carefully avoided voicing a single superior or deflating opinion, and he really couldn't understand why she was all wild-eyed and going over the edge screaming at him.

'Calm down,' Luc instructed steadily.

'Get away from that door or I'll throw something at you!' Star threatened.

'If wilful destruction gives you a juvenile thrill, go ahead,' Luc invited.

That provocative response sent such a flame of fury hurtling through Star she shuddered again. 'You're worse than a revolving door—'

'A revolving...door?' Stunning dark eyes rested on her with galling cool. 'Come on, don't leave me in suspense, *mon ange*. In what way do I remind you of a revolving door?'

'One minute you're there, the next you're not and then you're back again...you keep changing your mind and my head's *spinning!*' Star cried in shaking condemnation. 'I don't think you know what you want, but the minute I start wanting you back, you push me away again—'

'Control yourself,' Luc commanded.

'Control myself?' Star echoed, a whole octave higher. 'Gosh, that's a good one! Control yourself, but don't do it in bed. Do you think I want to end up a buttoned-down control freak like you are? I don't think you even *know* what goes on inside your own stupid head. I think around me you're totally controlled by your over-active male hormones! And you don't like that, do you? That gives me a certain power, doesn't it? And that annoys the *hell* out of you, Luc Sarrazin!'

She saw the sheer rage in his eyes and it went to her head like pure alcohol, because at last she had hit home and, if not hurt, had outraged him, which was probably as close as she could get to getting a rise out of Luc. In an abrupt movement, he stepped away from the door.

Assuming he was backing off, shocked rigid by the kind of verbal attack he had never dreamt of receiving from her corner, and feeling incredibly triumphant, Star sashayed out through the door. She paused then, and sent him a shimmering glance of naked incitement over one slight shoulder. 'And it didn't take me to be tall, blonde and sophisticated either, did it? That gets you most of all, doesn't it?'

'If you want to hear what I really think, keep on talking,' Luc ground out.

Star moved out into the hall and turned back again. 'I bet you could have swallowed me as a wife if I'd—'

'Shut up?' Luc slotted in rawly.

'No, if I'd been legitimate, rich and real snobby, you'd have thought I was really special!'

'Would your mother still have been part of the deal?'

'You pig...how dare you insult my mother?' she launched at him in a tempest of renewed fury.

Luc strode forward and just swept her up off her feet into his arms. 'Now where did you find an insult in such a simple question?' he probed, angling a razor-edged smile of grim amusement down at her confused face as he strode for the stairs.

'Put me down, Luc—'

'So that I can chase you all round one of the largest chateaux in the Loire? You must *really* think I am stupid, *mon ange*.'

'I think you're very stupid thinking that a caveman display of brute male strength is likely to silence and subdue me back into doormat mould!'

Luc said nothing, but his jawline took on an even more aggressive slant as he carted her up the stairs and across the landing.

'I hope you put your back out doing this!' Star goaded, wanting him to react again.

'In spite of a temper that would grace a fishwife, you don't weigh any more than a doll.' Shouldering open the door of his bedroom, Luc kicked it shut again behind them, crossed the room and tumbled her down on the bed in a heap. 'But if you get me mad enough, I'm not so buttoned down that I can't match you!'

Righting herself into a sitting position, Star slung back her head and directed a scornful glance at the tall dark male standing over her. 'What did you bring me up here for? An argument where the staff are less likely to hear us?'

Backing off several steps, Luc wrenched off his tie and pitched his jacket down on the floor.

That very unexpected development grabbed Star's entire attention. 'If you think for one moment that I have any intention of letting you—'

'*Letting* me?' Luc queried with an insolent appraisal that was so blisteringly confident it made her teeth grit. 'You'd let me have you in a thunderstorm, with lightning hitting the ground round us and a full orchestra playing beside us.'

'Why, you—'

'And you wouldn't notice the storm or the music because you would be *that* lost in what I can make you feel,' Luc derided, ripping off his shirt with such impatience that several buttons went skimming in all directions. 'And you call my hormones over-active? Even before I married you, you were eating me alive with the strength of your desire for me.'

'I never once approached you that way!' Star raged back at him, her cheeks red as fire.

'Approach me? What would you need to approach me for when your eyes did your craving for you? Then I thought you didn't realise what you were doing; now I suspect you knew *all* along.'

'I was a virgin!' Star proclaimed with embarrassed but infuriated reproach.

'There was nothing remotely virginal about the way you looked at me.'

'How many virgins have you tripped over?'

'*One* was quite enough,' Luc assured her wrathfully.

'It gave you a kick being lusted after, though, didn't it?' Star hissed like a spitting cat. 'I mean, you certainly did *not* avoid me—as you *should* have done if you didn't want to encourage me.'

'*Mais c'est insensé*…that's crazy! I assumed that the more you saw of me, the more you would appreciate that I was far too old for you and far too boring to be an object of such excessive adoration!' Luc slashed back at her.

'It was not excessive. I *loved* you! And you were only boring when you started rabbiting on about that stupid bank.'

A line of dark feverish colour rose over his taut cheek-bones at that less than tactful confirmation.

He could actually look *hurt*, Star registered in absolute total shock as she saw the shaken flash in his beautiful dark eyes. 'I mean, I didn't understand what you were talking about, so it was bound to be less than totally absorbing...and my mind used to drift away all the time, until I was just listening to the s-sound of your voice.'

The wobble in her own voice developed as he peeled off his trousers.

'Only a fool marries an airhead, so I got what I deserved,' Luc enunciated.

'I'm not an airhead...' But her mind was certainly drifting, Star acknowledged in deep shame. Not six feet from her stood the almost naked embodiment of every female fantasy come true, and her only fantasy—even *with* his clothes on. So with them off, barring an exceedingly cool pair of black silk boxer shorts, well, reasoning became a challenge. The twisting curl of heat low in her tummy made her go rigid with rejection.

'An airhead who thinks of nothing but sex,' Luc purred with awesome contempt. 'Who, after a separation of over eighteen months, went to bed with me again within an hour of my appearance back in her life.'

'Oh...*oh*!' Star gasped, the very oxygen squeezed from her lungs at that inexcusable taunt.

'OK, so I *asked*...but if you had any morals at all you would have said no to that proposition,' Luc condemned as he came down on the side of the bed. 'I was ashamed for you when I woke up the next morning.'

'The *next* morning?' Star forced a brittle laugh, so mad, so hurt she could happily have strangled the love of her life to death. 'Doesn't history repeat itself? Just like the only other night you ever spent with me. You're so mad you succumbed to me you punish *me* for it!'

'That is not true…' Luc emphasised that statement by pulling her round to face him. His dark eyes were forthright as flames on her surprised face. 'I got up the morning after our first night together and I looked down at you and you opened your eyes—'

'Gosh, how daring of me! Was I supposed to be hiding under the sheet in shame after spending the night with my own husband?'

Luc released his breath in a sharp hiss. 'I saw a teenager so besotted with me she couldn't see or think straight. I was angry, and ashamed that I had had so little control that I had taken advantage of you—'

'Don't tell me you felt like that!' Star wailed, aghast. 'It was wonderful…it's still a wonderful memory…and you didn't take advantage of me in any way!'

Luc studied her with unconcealed frustration. 'You don't see, do you? That morning, I really badly needed to look at you and see a grown woman, but all I could remember was the vulnerable little girl I first met in Mexico…' He hesitated, and frowned. 'It didn't strike me then that in some ways you'll probably never grow up, at least not in the way less passionate personalities do.'

'Oh, thanks a bundle.' Star exclaimed. 'Well, if you thought helping me to grow up was telling me to go off and experiment with boys my own age, I don't think much of your advice.'

'I said that in anger. Only you could have taken it so literally!' Luc gritted.

'How literally did you *want* me to take it?' Star asked with a teasing sidewise glance.

'You just never know when to quit, do you?' Without warning, Luc tugged her fully into his arms and stood up.

He held her fast and tumbled her back down onto the comfortable bed with him.

The heat of his big powerful body penetrated the fine silk of her dress. She quivered against him. She knew she wasn't going to say no. She knew *he* knew she wasn't going to say no either. Male amusement glimmered deep in his dark eyes and it made her want to slap him, but it didn't make her want to push him away.

'*D'accord*...OK, I gather I can assume that we're staying married.' Level dark eyes zeroed in on hers in enquiry.

Star tensed, lashes screening her gaze as she focused on a smooth brown shoulder instead. Stay married only for the sake of their children? Outside the bedroom he seemed to have as much grasp of *her* needs as the average block of solid wood. Or solid steel, she acknowledged, her weary mind running back over the enervating passage of events that had taken place during the past thirty-six hours. Her batteries required recharging. Yet Luc seemed able to take constant stress in his stride.

So damn him for making that statement which was really a direct question right now! Right now when there wasn't an atom of her treacherous body lacking contact with the awesome promise of his. Right now when she was suffering from this shockingly lowering need to cling and stop thinking and fighting. If she said no, that wasn't a sufficient reason to stay married, was he likely to chuck her out of bed?

Star rested her forehead down against Luc's shoulder. 'Talk about that later,' she mumbled.

'Why has your nightdress got a hood?' Luc enquired.

'It's a dress, Luc.'

Smoothly rearranging her so that she sat astride him, Luc eased it over her head and tossed it aside. 'Better off, than on, *mon ange*,' he mocked, but his intent gaze shimmered over the bare curves of her pouting breasts with smouldering appreciation.

Her face reddened as her nipples pinched into straining

tautness. Luc tensed and suddenly hauled her down to him. 'I'm so glad you're all argued out,' he groaned, closing his mouth hungrily to a thrusting pink peak.

As he did so, a wave of such intense excitement clenched Star that she stopped breathing. She shut her eyes, moaning as he caught the other bud between thumb and forefinger and gently tugged on her achingly responsive flesh. Her whole body was electrified with need as he rolled her over onto her back, skimming off her briefs with sure hands.

He scrutinised her with satisfied eyes. She opened her own, collided with that appraisal and snatched in a sob, just desperate for him to touch her again, and suddenly the amount of power he had over her weak physical self mortified her. 'Don't look at me like that—'

'I always get a high out of your response to me. Can't help it,' Luc muttered hoarsely, still scanning her slender naked curves with devouring attention. 'On your last stay here, I spent the entire time wondering, burning, fantasising…'

'About me?' Her sultry smile was as natural to her as breathing.

'And trying to work out what it was about you that got to me.' Luc ran a caressing hand down over her sensitive breasts, smiling slumbrously as her back arched.

'Oh…?' Her voice emerged strangled.

'You're very small, but you're in perfect proportion. Your eyes are a wonderful colour, and your mouth…when I look at your gorgeous mouth, I just get…' Luc framed the words thickly, sinking lower with every driven word as if the more he said, the more unbearable it became to resist that part of her.

She got the message when he kissed her with all the hunger she craved, but for a split second her brain got its act together and a solitary thought emerged. Luc was talking to her, Luc was *finally* talking to her, but it mightn't be a good idea to mention it because he probably didn't realise what he was doing. And then the primal thrust of his tongue inside her tender mouth just drove her wild. Her mind emptied as she held him to her, fingers laced in his hair, heart pounding in concert with his, the thrumming pulse-beat of desire running like a tightening hot wire through her slender length.

'You excite me beyond belief,' Luc muttered raggedly, pulling back from her to remove his boxer shorts.

Star blinked. My goodness, he was *still* talking. She gazed at him with slightly worried eyes and decided that it had to be stress that was making him talk so much. He came back to her, all rippling muscles and magnificence, and all-pervasive weakness radiated through her lower limbs. She reached up without even the guidance of thought and ran her palms down over the curling dark hair that hazed his pectorals, loving the heat and the roughness of him, the glorious differences that made him so male and made her feel so incredibly feminine.

He shuddered and crushed her eagerly parted lips under his, sensually exploring and tasting her until tiny little quaking tremors were rippling through her.

'You're so quiet,' Luc breathed, sounding almost disappointed, which she could not credit.

If he wanted intellectual stimulation, he was going the wrong way about it. 'I...I can't think when you're this close to me, Luc...I can only *feel*.'

And what Star was feeling was shivering, desperate impatience, her skin hot and tight, the terrible ache he could arouse with such ease sending taunting little throbs of frustration along every single nerve-ending.

'A man should take time making love to his wife.' Luc sent her a winging smile of pure devilment.

The combination of that smile flashing across his lean, dark, devastating face and that teasing reference to her as his wife shook her. He pulled her to him like a guy who had all the time in the world and who planned to enjoy making her wait. Her fingers bit fiercely into his shoulder, and he laughed in a way she had never heard him laugh with her before, and then he sealed her mouth again with his and the hunger took her in an explosive surge again.

He touched her in every place but the one place craving his touch. She discovered she had erogenous zones all over her. He let his sensual mouth nip at the extended line of her throat and she was convinced she would burst into flame. He licked her fingers and her very bones seemed to liquefy. He smoothed his palms with aching slowness along the outside of her slender thighs and she burned in absolute torment. And when he started shaping her squirming hips, she clawed him down to her in a tempestuous movement.

'If you don't…' she moaned.

And then he did, and nothing from that point on could have wrenched her from the grip of such torturous excitement. Not thunder, not lightning, not even a full orchestra. Sounds escaped her that she didn't recognise as her own, and she twisted and she writhed until at last he came over her.

And Luc was trembling too then, dampness sheening his golden skin, the hands that spread her beneath him taut and impatient, dark eyes burnished with raw desire. He entered her in a hungry surging thrust. She cried out loud, out of control, loving it, loving him with such fevered intensity that the pleasure seemed more than she could bear. And as he drove her deeper into that pleasure with long, hard strokes, she felt the great gathering ultimate surge taking her in its hold and just let go, gasping, shuddering, sobbing out his name at the height of ecstasy.

'I think, *mon ange*…' Luc groaned indolently into her hair. 'I think I shall adapt to being *really* married with remarkable enthusiasm.'

She shifted indolently against him, enfolded by the most marvellous sense of peace and satiation. Lifting his head, Luc gazed down at her abstracted expression and he laughed softly. 'You're still out of it.'

Out of everything, she conceded happily as he traced the relaxed fullness of her reddened lips with a fingertip and gave her the sort of megawatt smile that made her heart sing. 'Just keep on smiling at me…'

'I believe I can definitely promise you that.' His dark drawl husky with sensual amusement, Luc rolled over into a cooler patch of the tumbled bed, but he kept her welded to him with one powerfully possessive arm and covered her mouth very softly with his again.

It felt as if the whole world stood still while he kissed her. Glorious contentment enveloped Star. She closed her arms round him in helpless hunger, revelling in the damp, hard feel of his relaxed length and knowing that she already wanted him again.

Lifting his tousled head, Luc scanned her with stunning dark eyes ablaze with the same awareness. 'It's hard to believe that in the early hours of this morning. I was angry and drunk and climbing the walls with sexual frustration…and look at us now.'

Yes, look at us now, Star suddenly thought, tensing at the reminder of that upsetting confrontation during the night. It was as if Luc had pressed a panic button inside her head. Luc seemed to be suggesting that now everything was sorted, as it were. He thought, he had actually just assumed, that he had got what he wanted and that she had now agreed to stay married to him. And why *shouldn't* he have made that assumption? Hadn't she just fallen at abandoned speed back into bed with him again?

'For the sake of our children,' he had drawled piously, when he had stated the case for finally making their marriage a real and binding commitment. And didn't she still love him? Wasn't this probably the very most Luc was ever likely to offer her? What was she holding out for? Red roses and romance? Chance would be a fine thing! But how much could she even *trust* in what Luc was saying right now?

'You know…' she said uneasily, pulling away from him in a move that took an amount of will-power that embarrassed her. 'Only last night you were talking like you hated me...'

Faint colour surfaced over his hard cheekbones and he frowned. 'I still believed that the twins had been fathered by some other man! You never put yourself in my place, *mon ange.*'

No, now that he said it, she had to admit that she hadn't ever tried. But then she had never managed to work out what went on inside Luc's head. However, she suspected that when his emotions became involved Luc's sense of proportion and his pure logic went out of the window, leaving him vulnerable. How else did she explain an overwhelmingly practical guy who, on the basis of a goodbye note, had had the moat and the lake dragged for her body?

'But ever since you tracked me down all you've been talking about is divorcing me. It was like it was a real mission with you...'

'So *that* is what is worrying you. But naturally my priorities have changed,' Luc countered without hesitation. 'We have the twins to consider now. They need their mother just as much as their father. You and I both enjoyed less than idyllic childhoods. By staying together we support each other as parents and we can ensure that our children enjoy a different experience.'

Star's heart was steadily sinking. She had put him on the spot again when he hadn't been expecting it, but couldn't he just have lied and pretended that *she* figured in this reconciliation as something more than the mother of his children? No, she was better off with that honesty, she decided miserably. Even she couldn't romanticise deeper meanings into words and phrases like 'priorities' and 'supporting each other as parents'.

Luc was determined to hang onto Venus and Mars. First he had softened her up with the threat of a custody battle, then he had tried to talk her back into a marriage he had previously been keen to escape. All for the benefit of the twins. But children and good intentions were not enough to hold a marriage together. Why on earth was Luc the logical being so *illogical*? Her head whirled. It was as if they had suddenly switched characters. *She* was supposed to be the one who chased idealistic windmills; *he* was supposed to be the one grounded in the solid rock of realistic expectations!

Star dropped her head and murmured heavily, 'I think we should just take stock of our marriage at the end of the summer…and not make any hard and fast decisions before then.'

Luc threw back the sheet and sprang out of bed.

That got her attention all right. She watched him hauling on his boxer shorts and then snatching up the chinos lying on a nearby chair. His long, smooth brown back expressed hostility in violent waves. In the space of ten seconds the atmosphere had churned up and charged like dynamite ready to explode.

'Luc?' Star prompted apprehensively.

Luc swung back, dark eyes grim. 'Explain exactly what you mean by that suggestion. I want to be sure I haven't misunderstood.'

'Well, we just see how we get on over the summer—'

'You keep your options open until then?' Raw incredulity edged his dark accented drawl.

Star nodded. That way she wouldn't get her hopes up too much. That way if he discovered he couldn't hack being married to her, she would be prepared and she wouldn't be quite so hurt.

Studying a point slightly to one side of her, Luc breathed in very deep, so deep she could see his impressive chest expanding. '*Rien à faire*…nothing doing!'

She stiffened. 'But—'

With a slashing motion of one powerful hand, Luc silenced her. 'When you went to bed with me again, you *knew* that I believed you had agreed to my terms!'

Star quickly dropped her head again, wincing, wishing he

wasn't quite so clever. 'I just wanted you so much…can't you accept that?'

'You're my wife and you're behaving like a wanton little slut!'

'You don't mean that,' she told him, looking up hopefully but meeting hard, challenging eyes across the depth of the room and shrinking.

'I heard you telling Rory you loved him last night,' Luc ground out.

'Oh…' Her mind occupied with something which was to her way of thinking much more pressing, Star said, 'Are you about to apologise for calling me a slut?'

'Not on my deathbed!' Luc roared, which seemed fairly comprehensive.

'Fine…this dialogue is over until you say sorry.' Beneath his arrested gaze, Star flopped back on the pillows and shut her eyes.

'Rory was not on your mind that night in England…*and* he was a very distant memory not ten minutes ago, when you were having a hell of a good time under me!'

Star whispered frigidly, 'And when you were having a hell of a good time *over* me. So that leaves us about equal.'

'How can you be so crude?' Luc had the nerve to sound genuinely shocked.

'I just learnt it from you. But at least I have never in my life eavesdropped on someone else's private phone call…' It was a lie: on their wedding night she had listened to him call Gabrielle and say he was coming over. That recollection just choked her. 'But I love Rory like a friend…OK?'

'No, it is not OK!' Luc thundered back at her. 'You will have no further contact with him. And if you think for one moment that I intend to be put on trial as a stud for the summer, you are out of your crazy mind!'

Star felt frozen from neck to toe. She looked up at the superb ornate ceiling, exhaustion creeping over her. 'I wouldn't worry about that if I were you. I have no plans to ever sleep with you again, Luc Sarrazin. Are you going to apologise? Because if you're not, you can leave.'

As the silence lingered, Luc closed his eyes and counted to ten, then to twenty. This terrible rage she evoked. He felt as if he was coming apart at the seams. He felt gutted. He strode into the dressing room and flipped the door shut. She *loved* Rory like a friend? She had to have slept with the guy. Of course she had! All those months when he himself had been... He just could not stand to think about that, rammed that thought train back down into his subconscious. It leapt out again like an evil genie. Who was the smartass who'd told her to experiment?

Star wakened a couple of hours later, amazed that she had just dropped off to sleep. There was a note on the pillow beside her. She lifted it with a frown, everything that had happened between her and Luc flooding back.

'Urgent appointment to keep. Sorry, Luc,' the note ran.

He was gone. She had chased him back to Paris. Her eyes stung like mad with tears. It had been thirty-six hours of mostly hell, but she couldn't bear him that far away from her—especially after a violent row. All she had done was fight with him. What had got into her? He couldn't stand scenes. All right, so it hadn't been the most tempting invitation to stay married, but she could have been more tactful. He had been shocked when she'd announced that she would prefer to go for the trial reconciliation rather than the for ever and for ever challenge.

She didn't even have the number of his mobile phone. She didn't even know when he was coming back. Six lousy words, and one of those his own name. She buried her face in the pillow and sobbed her heart out.

CHAPTER EIGHT

By THREE that afternoon, Star was dry-eyed. As Luc had promised, all the rest of her possessions had arrived and she was in the midst of organising a workroom for herself.

She had picked a room on the ground floor, where the light was particularly good and the view from the windows inspirational. The shop which had bought her first small embroidered canvases had indicated an interest in seeing more of her pictures. As she didn't know what was likely to be happening between her and Luc at the end of the summer, she needed to be every bit as disciplined at forging a career as an artist as she had been at home. The ability to be self-supporting, whether it was necessary or not, was important to her self-esteem.

Her body had a slight, definite ache, which was as strong a reminder of Luc's infuriating absence as it was of her own weak physical self. Of course Luc had been furious with her. Luc always thought he knew best. But he didn't necessarily know what was best for *her*. Luc could be terrifyingly self-sufficient, and she needed more than she had naively wanted eighteen months earlier. She hadn't even understood that herself until he had suggested staying together solely for the twins' benefit.

Granted, Luc wasn't *ever* going to fall madly in love with her: no longer did she wish for the moon. But if Luc couldn't love her, he had to respect her, care for her well-being and stop treating her like an overgrown child who couldn't be trusted to express a sensible opinion of her own.

A maid appeared at the door to tell her that there was a call for her.

Star swept up the phone.

'It's Luc.'

Star stiffened, still furious at the unfeeling way he had vanished while she was asleep. 'I know. Don't tell me. You're too busy to come home for dinner?'

'I'm afraid that I somehow overlooked an emergency meeting on the current stockmarket crisis—'

She didn't believe him. He never overlooked anything. He just didn't want to come home. 'So where's the meeting?' she enquired very coolly.

'Singapore.'

Singapore? Aghast, she studied her own white-knuckled grip on the phone. How many hours did it take to fly to Singapore? Was he even likely to make it back for dinner tomorrow evening? She didn't think so. The fight went out of her. She went limp

'It isn't possible for someone else to attend in my place,' Luc imparted with audible tension. 'I know that this is a case of extremely bad timing as far as *we* are concerned, but I have a duty and responsibility as Chairman to attend this conference. I'll be home next week—'

'Next week?' Her horror escaped her this time in a shrill exclamation. She clamped a frantic hand to her parted lips, furious at her loss of control.

'I would prefer to be spending time with you and the children. Please understand that sometimes I don't have a choice,' Luc breathed stiffly.

'Oh, don't worry about us. We'll be fine, and I'm sure you're really busy, so I won't keep you. Have a nice time!'

She sank down on the nearest seat, feeling as if Luc had yanked the very ground from beneath her feet. Next week. All those days to be got through. There were twenty-four hours in every day, sixty minutes in every hour. What was the matter with her? She had managed without Luc for a long time. All right, so she hadn't been happy, but she had stopped feeling dependent. It made her mad that the passage of barely two days could make such a difference.

* * *

Luc phoned at odd hours during the following week.

There were awkward silences. Then one or both of them would rush into speech, usually to say, or in his case ask, something about Venus and Mars. The phone was a business aid to Luc. He didn't chat. He didn't share the experiences of his day. And Star was too mortified to press him on the latter subject after her pretty much unforgivable crack about how bored she had once been when he mentioned anything relating to the Sarrazin bank.

A little over eighteen months ago she had thought she was so mature for her age too. Now she was looking back and wincing for her younger self, appreciating how much she *had* matured since becoming a mother. Before the twins' birth she had been as self-absorbed as most teenagers. Luc's work-aholic schedule had just made her resent the Sarrazin bank and she hadn't ever attempted to understand anything he tried to explain.

The day before Luc was due to return, Star took the twins into the woods for a walk and a picnic. It was a heavenly afternoon. Drowsing early summer heat seeped down through the tree canopy into the grassy glade where Star had spread a rug. With the twins dozing in their pram, Star was in a dreamy daze when she heard a slight sound and lifted her head. Her expressive eyes widened, her throat constricting.

Luc came to a halt several feet away. In an elegant cream suit that accentuated the stunning darkness of his hair and the vibrant gold of his skin, he looked drop-dead gorgeous. Her mouth ran dry and her heart leapt.

'Luc…how on earth…? I mean…I wasn't expecting you!' Scrambling up, the folds of her many-shaded long green skirt fluttering round her slender frame, she surged off the rug in her bare feet, only to jerk to a sudden halt about eighteen inches from him as she recalled her original intent to greet his return with frozen cool.

'No, don't spoil that welcome!' His amusement uncon-

cealed as he recognised her dismay, Luc reached out and
urged her the rest of the way to him.

A lean hand splaying to her slim hips, to pin her in place,
he gazed down at her, lush lashes screening all but a dark
glimmer of his eye. 'I think you missed me—'

'I was just so surprised to see you standing there. I got a
fright!' Star's cheeks were red as fire.

'With those eyes, you can't lie…you really can't lie to me,
mon ange,' Luc chided, his other hand curving to her chin
to push up her face, his fingers slowly sliding into her hair.
'And why should you lie?'

The touch of his hand on her sun-warmed skin sent a wave
of undeniable awareness tremoring down her taut spinal cord.
She fought the sensation with all her might, only to succumb
to the sudden passionate force of Luc's mouth possessing
hers.

After a week of deprivation, he had the same effect on her
as a flame on dynamite. Her whole body leapt in sensual
shock. She closed her hands over his shoulders to keep herself upright as she leant into him, the heat and strength of
his hard, muscular frame a powerful enticement. Wildly excited by the taste of him, she closed her arms around him,
quivering as she registered his potent arousal.

Suddenly Luc dragged his mouth from hers, bracing his
hands momentarily on her shoulders to steady her, and
laughed softly. 'We have an audience…'

He strode away. Blinking in bemusement, Star spun round.
Luc was now hunkered down by the pram, all his attention
directed at Venus, who was holding out her arms and making
little excitable noises of welcome. Feeling like a third wheel,
Star stiffened and bit her lower lip.

'Star…' Luc extended his hand.

'What?'

'I have time to make up with you, but time to make up
with our son and daughter as well,' he murmured smoothly.

Her face burned like a house fire. She had never been so

grateful that he wasn't looking at her. If she had been sixteen, she'd have stormed off in furious embarrassment. Four years older, she compressed her lips and approached the pram. Tugging her down beside him, Luc curved a strong arm round her.

'This is what I want them to see. You and I together and relaxed,' he shared softly. 'Aside of weddings and funerals, I never saw my parents together. They despised each other. If they had to communicate they used the phone. I thought that was normal. I thought all families lived like that...each of them entirely separate under the same roof.'

Her discomfiture was forgotten. The images Luc evoked chilled her.

'That's why I want something better for our children,' Luc continued in the same level tone. 'Because I know the cost of getting something less. I'm not prepared to *play* at being married while you make up your mind about what you want to do.'

'I wasn't suggesting we—'

'You *were*...and if you start out with the belief that it's all right to fail, failure becomes that much more likely.' Releasing her from his light hold, Luc vaulted back upright.

'That's not how I see it.' Her aquamarine eyes frustrated, she scrambled up.

Luc gave her a cloaked scrutiny. 'I won't be put on trial.'

'I'm not putting you on trial, for goodness' sake!'

His eyes glittered like ice-fire in a shaft of sunlight. 'I've already lost out on the first year of my children's lives and yet you're expecting me to spend the next few months wondering whether we're likely to end up fighting over them in court!'

Taken aback by that statement, Star swallowed uncertainly.

'And not only that,' Luc continued with glacial cool, 'At the same time you actually expect me to behave as if our marriage is normal and treat you as my wife—a bond which requires a sense of trust and security. What do you think I am? A split personality?'

'How long did it take you to work out that argument?' Star asked with helpless curiosity, eyes now wide with wonderment.

Disconcerted by that offbeat question, and by the way she was studying him, Luc frowned.

Star gave a slow, rueful shake of her bright head. 'Never mind. I have to admit that I'm torn between resentment and admiration. You've made a very good point and pretty much trashed my argument.'

Without another word, she threaded her feet into her sandals and then whisked up the rug and carefully folded it. She planted the rug into his surprised hands and then, retracing her steps, wheeled the pram in the direction of the path. She glanced back, noting Luc was still poised like a devastatingly handsome statue in the same spot.

'Aren't you coming?' she asked in surprise.

'What you just said…' Luc drawled as he strode onto the path. 'What did it…*mean*?'

'I'll tell you when I work it out. Mmm…' she sighed with a sunny smile. 'I love the smell of the woods.'

'Star, we need to sort this out—'

'Relax…unwind…loosen your tie,' Star urged pleadingly.

He wanted to organise their marriage along the strict lines of his daily schedule. Nothing unexpected, nothing outside normal boundaries, everything under his rational, structured control. He couldn't help himself. His brain was like a steel trap. And arguing with him was a waste of time. She wasn't about to be browbeaten into changing her mind on the spur of the moment. She was a lateral thinker who worked on gut instinct. Luc was just going to have to accept that.

When they got back to the chateau, they entertained the twins for an hour. After that, Venus and Mars had their tea and Bertille helped Star to bathe them. By the time the children were tucked into their cots Star was hungry, and, since

Luc was now home again, she went to change for dinner. Clad in a floaty lemon dress that skimmed her ankles, she went downstairs and joined Luc in the drawing room.

To her surprise, Luc wasn't wearing his usual formal evening dress. Dressed in beautifully cut khaki chinos and a toning shirt, he looked very elegant, yet very much more casual than she was accustomed to seeing him. In that split-second first encounter with his brilliant dark gaze, her tummy clenched and her pulses quickened. Her awareness of his devastating masculinity intensified to a degree that made her suddenly self-conscious.

'Where's your dinner jacket?' she muttered in a rush to fill in the silence, shifting from one foot to the other, her cheeks warming as she hurriedly lowered her eyes from the downright lure of his.

'Do you remember telling me that when I wore a dinner jacket I reminded you of the men who appear in old black and white movies?' Luc enquired gently. 'Since then, for some reason, I've never felt quite the same about dressing up for dinner.'

'Well, times do change, although they never did *here*, did they?' Star started talking in mile-a-minute mode. 'Your father was a real old stick-in-the-mud for living the way your ancestors did. The last time I stayed here it was like I'd strayed back into the eighteenth century and was living history!'

Luc scanned her simple dress with its delicate embroidery. 'But in spite of that, you're now dressing for dinner.'

Star just grinned; she couldn't help it: it was just typical that they should be out of step. But as she connected with his magnetic dark eyes a second time, that thought drifted from her again, more elemental responses taking over. All she really wanted was to be in his arms, and she felt she ought to have more control over herself.

'You do look gorgeous in that dress,' Luc extended softly. 'And it's going to be the perfect foil for my present.'

'Present?'

Luc swept a gift-wrapped box from the table behind him and settled it into her hands.

In genuine surprise, Star sat down hurriedly to open the box. When she lifted out a chakra necklace, she studied it in total shock. She only recognised what it was because she had once seen one in a book. Each different gemstone and crystal had been exquisitely cut and framed in intricate settings, the whole joined by delicate gold links.

Stunned, Star looked up and stared at Luc in amazement. 'It's just *gorgeous*...where did you get it?'

'I had it made for you while I was in Singapore. A practitioner skilled in the healing qualities of crystals and gemstones helped me to decide what to include.'

Star slowly swallowed. 'B-but you—'

Luc touched the first gemstone. 'Amber for calm, amethyst for spiritual peace, aquamarine for communication...' he enumerated steadily. 'Azurite to help you find your life path and to trust in your intuition, topaz to protect you through life changes, opal for meditation, tourmaline to heal past traumas, lapis lazuli to change negative views into positive ones...and a rose quartz pendulum for powerful healing energy.'

'I just can't believe this...' Star mumbled, examining each gem with close interest backed by growing appreciation and excitement at the meaning of so very personalised a present. 'This means so much to me, Luc...and that you should have taken the trouble, made the effort when you don't even *believe* in—'

'There is a scientific basis to your convictions. Now that I know that, I can handle the concept better.'

'You mean you don't think I'm a crackpot any more?' Star asked hopefully.

'I never said you were a crackpot.'

'It must have cost you a fortune...not that that counts for anything, with your wealth...but this is just one of those very, very special gifts that speaks so loud...' At that point, Star got up and flung her arms round him, her heart singing like a thousand violins reaching a crescendo. 'You are turning into a really wonderful guy, Luc!'

His arms full of Star, Luc frowned. *Turning into?* From a rat into a wonderful guy. It was a meteoric rise, he conceded. He had known that she would be really surprised by the necklace, but he was astonished that a gift had the power to inspire her with such an emotional response. But then she was very impressionable. Recalling the amount of cool calculation that had gone into that necklace, he suppressed a very slight pang of conscience.

'Put it on for me,' Star whispered.

Taking the necklace from her, Luc undid the catch. She turned round and bent her head for him, felt the cool weight of the jewellery and then, in shock, the hard, sensual promise of his lips pressing to the exposed nape of her neck. Her knees wobbled and every nerve-ending just seemed to sizzle, making her gasp.

'You are so deliciously responsive, Madame Sarrazin,' Luc teased huskily above her head as she fell back into the waiting circle of his arms, every inch of her so tormentingly aware of that lean, hard frame of his that she blushed all over.

He held her fast, the warm, sexy scent of him engulfing her, wiping out all self-discipline. Instinctively she pushed back against him, and he vented a roughened groan at that contact. 'Luc...' she framed with a desperate little shiver.

'Relax...' he urged slumbrously, effortlessly in control when she already felt weak with physical need.

He let his hands roam with sure expertise up over the straining thrust of her urgently sensitive breasts and she jerked and moaned, arching back in a fever of trembling excitement. It had only been a week but it felt like a hundred years since she had last felt his touch.

With a ragged sigh, Luc turned her back to him and stole

one devouring kiss full of a hunger that more than matched her own. Then he dragged his mouth free again and held her tight against him until the fever inside her had subsided to a more bearable level. 'Touching you wasn't the brightest idea…' His own breathing was fractured, his deep voice uneven. 'Particularly not when the bell's already gone for dinner.'

Star hadn't even heard it sounding.

Luc set her back from him with determined but gentle hands. 'Our chef always pushes the boat out when I've been abroad,' he shared ruefully. 'There's probably five courses coming our way. He'll be mortally offended if we don't at least *try* to eat some of it.'

Star touched her necklace several times during the meal which followed. She noticed nothing she ate. She couldn't take her eyes off Luc. She felt buoyant, and full of hope for the future. Luc had used his imagination on her behalf. He had made a real effort to move beyond his own conventional boundaries. Considerable care had gone into the selection of those particular gemstones. And he had done all that purely to please her. From a guy who was at least ninety per cent preoccupied with banking most of the time that was a really impressive gesture, and it touched her to the heart.

They got as far as the dessert during dinner. Then Luc pushed his plate away and held his hand out to her. Her face hot with colour but her body hot with wild anticipation, Star rose from the table to join him.

'Are you feeling happy?' she asked him as they crossed the big hall hand in hand for the very first time.

'It's not a concept I've explored since childhood. What does it feel like?' Luc enquired with amusement.

'I think you'd have to be really *unhappy* before you could appreciate what the reverse feels like.'

'Are you planning to sleep on the sofa tonight?' Brilliant dark eyes encountered and held hers.

'No…' Star muttered breathlessly.

'I am experiencing happiness at this moment, *ma cherie*,' Luc drawled with unconcealed mockery.

Star tensed with sudden discomfiture at the strength of her desire for him. 'A lot of things are more important than sex, Luc—'

'Not to most men,' Luc slotted in softly.

'Is that like a guy thing?'

'Definitely. And, speaking as a male who only planned to marry after his fiftieth birthday—'

Star stopped dead and surveyed him in amazement. 'But why?'

'I didn't want to risk wasting the best years of my life in a bad marriage,' Luc admitted without hesitation. 'It makes sense. Think about it.'

Star didn't want to think about it. She was appalled by such a pessimistic outlook. 'You can't plan stuff like that, Luc.'

'Not with you in the vicinity,' he conceded.

'But didn't it even cross your mind that you might fall madly in love?'

'In lust, yes…in love, no.'

'But I always feel good when I'm in love…well, most of the time,' Star adjusted ruefully.

Sudden silence reigned.

Star glanced at Luc's hard profile and sighed, her eyes veiling. 'You're not comfortable with this conversation, are you?'

Luc tightened his grip on her slender fingers as they began to slide inexorably from his. 'I think the less you think about love the happier we will be,' he stated with flat conviction.

A faraway look of regret in her eyes, Star realised that she was *still* wishing for the moon, and that Luc had just forced her dreams into yet another crash landing. Only a week ago she had been telling herself that she had come to terms with the fact that Luc didn't believe in romantic love. But it was hard to feel optimistic about a potential future with a husband who didn't love her. Particularly when they were such different kinds of people. How loyal would he be to a wife he didn't love?

Now rigid with seething tension, Luc removed his gaze abruptly from her preoccupied face. 'I've got some work to do,' he told her flatly, and released her hand.

Literally exploded out of her anxious thoughts, Star stilled in complete confusion to watch Luc stride away from her and head back down the magnificent staircase again.

She gripped the banister. 'I could keep you company...?'

At the foot of the stairs, Luc swung round, his lean, hard features icily sardonic.

Shrivelled by that look, Star stepped back, the warmth inside her evaporating beneath that chill. 'I guess you don't need company...'

One minute they had been heading for bed, excitement in the air—well, in *her* air anyway. No longer did she feel qualified to say how Luc had been feeling—but the next minute she had become as undesirable as cold tea. Had she said something which annoyed him? She had started talking about love. She groaned, thoroughly irritated with a tongue which frequently ran ahead of her brain in Luc's company. Why did he have to be so touchy? Not just touchy, she conceded heavily, Luc had seem derisive...*repelled*?

Was that her fault? What made a guy go from keen to cold? Too much eagerness? Had Luc been in the act of dragging her off to bed only because she herself had made it so painfully obvious that she could hardly wait for him to make love to her again? Star cringed at that suspicion. No doubt after a couple of sexual encounters she no longer possessed quite the same 'wild' appeal. In fact, maybe now that Luc suspected that in all likelihood she was *always* going to be around, her stock in the desirability stakes had sunk a great deal lower.

After an hour's wakeful twisting and turning in a bed which seemed far too big and far too empty for her, Star sat up with the sense of having finally penetrated the mystery of Luc's behaviour with an explanation that was very slightly less humiliating. For goodness' sake, what an idiot she was! She remembered him admitting that he hadn't planned to marry until he was at least fifty. Now she knew what was wrong. All of a sudden Luc had felt *trapped*, twenty years ahead of his time. In presenting him with two children she had deprived him of the freedom and female variety that all young, sexually active males supposedly cherished. An extra twenty years was a long term to serve for not using contraception, she allowed miserably.

Seated at his desk, Luc sank a brandy in one long, unappreciative gulp. And she called *him* insensitive! He had never been the sensitive type, but Star was getting to him on levels he did not wish to explore. He saw that wistful, yearning expression on her face afresh. His anger got colder and deadlier. Or was it anger? He realised in some surprise that he felt bitter. He felt very, very bitter.

From below her lashes, while pretending to still be asleep, Star watched Luc emerge from the bathroom the next morning.

Stark naked, he was towelling dry his hair. A sensation akin to a tightening knot tugged low in the pit of her stomach. Feeling like a voyeur, she shut her eyes tight in shame. She recalled telling him that there were a lot more important things than sex and decided it was time she learned to practise what she preached. She didn't know what time Luc had finally come to bed. By that stage she had given up hope of him ever appearing and she had dozed off.

'I know you're awake,' Luc remarked lazily.

Her lashes practically hit her eyebrows. *'How?'*

A vibrant smile curved Luc's mouth. 'I spoke and you took the bait!'

She laughed, but it was a challenge. At that instant, his dark, vibrant magnetism just took her breath away.

Wearing only a pair of boxer shorts, Luc strolled across to the bed and sank lithely down on the edge, all bronzed skin, rippling muscles and tangible energy. He handed her a gold credit card and a fat wad of francs. 'You need to do some serious shopping today.'

'Why?'

'Surprise...' His dark eyes gleamed. 'But shop for somewhere hot.'

She sat up with a jerk. 'Are we going away?'

'Late afternoon. You, me, the twins.'

Very slowly Star nodded; she was totally stunned. Luc had once had the same view of holidays as Scrooge had had of Christmas. What was making him so volatile? Why all these inexplicable changes of mood? Last night he had been grim as hell when he'd turned away from her in a very hurtful rejection, and *now*? Like a guy on a mission, he radiated charisma and smiles.

'For a couple of weeks,' Luc added casually.

'What about the bank?'

'I'm tearing myself away from it...but I have to go in today to tie up a few loose ends...OK, *mon ange*?' Lowering his dark head, Luc crushed her parted lips with hungry brevity beneath his, and then rose with unconcealed reluctance again.

'OK...' she said breathlessly.

As he got dressed, Luc listened with the utmost contentment to Star singing off-key in the shower. To think he had actually been apprehensive about the reception he might receive! Storming off last night had been a major misjudgement, he acknowledged. If she had done the same thing to him, he would have been ready to strangle her. Fortunately, Star was happily distracted by the idea of a holiday.

And around dawn Luc had finally seen the error of his ways. Under no circumstances was he prepared to wait until the end of the summer to discover their ultimate fate as a family. And the solution to that problem was so simple that

Luc could not credit he had taken so long to see it. He had to *make* Star fall in love with him again. Then a nuclear bomb wouldn't shift her from his side...

Star spent the morning shopping in Nantes.

In a medieval side-street, she found a fabulous baby shop, and kitted Venus and Mars out with substantial new wardrobes. When cost didn't have to be considered, she discovered to her delight, she could shop at supersonic speed. She bought lingerie by the handful, swimwear and new toe-post sandals in five different colours. In quick succession she went on to purchase T-shirts, two short skirts, five long floaty ones she couldn't choose between, three new dresses and canvas shoes. Stocking up on suncream, a new straw hat and a pair of leopard print sunglasses completed the trip.

With Bertille's organisational ability to hand, and the wonderful knowledge that she could pack the kitchen sink if she so desired, Star had closed the last suitcase and had changed into a fashionably short lemon lace-lined skirt, teamed with a sequinned white T-shirt, when the internal phone rang to inform her that she had a visitor waiting to see her, a Mr Martin. Rory...Rory was here in *France*?

Star flew down the stairs like the wind. Rory was in the hall, looking amazingly elegant in white jeans and a designer T-shirt with a striped cotton sweater casually knotted round his slim shoulders.

As Luc strolled through the imposing front door of his ancestral home, wondering who owned the Porsche with the British registration parked out front, he was just in time to see his wife hurl herself joyously into Rory's arms.

'What a brilliant surprise!' With the ease of long friendship, Star gripped the young blond man's arms, stretched up to kiss his cheek and then held him back from her to subject him to a long, exaggerated appraisal before sounding a low wolf-whistle of admiration. 'Wow! Love those sexy white jeans...don't you look like a really cool dude?'

Rory grinned. 'I brought the Porsche Cabriolet too—'

'Poser!' she mocked, her aquamarine eyes dancing. 'And to think you made me travel round in an ancient old rust-bucket because you didn't want your workmates to know that you were a rich kid.'

'Now, come on, Star...the Morris is a classic British car.'

'I have definitely missed you. Why are you skiving off work and over in France?' she demanded cheerfully.

'I'm supposed to be checking that my parents' villa at Cap d'Antibes is in order for the end of the month... I was worried about you and the twins,' he admitted abruptly.

'Didn't I tell you you didn't need to worry?' Star sighed guiltily. 'Luc and I are—'

'Deliriously happy,' Luc's heavy accented drawl slotted in to spell out.

Star whirled round with a huge but surprised smile. 'Luc, you're home! Come and meet Rory...*properly* this time! He's got to be my best friend in the world.'

From a distance of ten feet, Luc stared bleakly at the young blond man. Rory advanced half a step and then stilled again, acknowledging his host's presence with an uneasy nod.

Star focused on Luc. It struck her that he was remarkably pale, his slashing cheekbones taut. 'Luc, are you—?'

'Look, I'll call in on the way back from the Cap on Sunday.' Rory began.

Star grimaced. 'Oh, heck, we won't be here, Rory. In fact—'

'In just under ten minutes we have to leave,' Luc advanced without the slightest shade of regret.

'Gosh, it's a good thing I got my packing done so quick,' Star muttered in surprise, and some embarrassment. 'We're going away for a couple of weeks, Rory.'

'Possibly even longer,' Luc qualified.

Star glanced at him in bewilderment. 'But, Luc...what about the bank?'

'With a computer, I can work anywhere,' Luc asserted with sardonic bite.

Rory glanced uncomfortably at Star. 'Could I just say hi to the twins before I go?'

'Of course you can!' Star headed for the stairs. 'I feel so awful that you can't stay longer.'

'Luc is a very possessive guy,' Rory whispered on the landing. 'He really doesn't like me being here—'

'Nonsense,' Star said loyally. 'Luc was just surprised to see you, that's all.'

'You seem so happy...'

'I am. So you shouldn't be worrying about me.'

'I went on the pull, like you suggested. I'm going clubbing with a brunette this week,' Rory informed her.

Star grinned approval. 'You could never do anything like that with me because I had the twins...'

'And you'd never agree to a babysitter,' Rory added with a thoughtful frown.

After a brief visit with Venus and Mars, Star walked Rory back out to his Porsche.

'I'll call back at the end of the month. Hell, I nearly forgot... Yesterday, Juno phoned me at work in a real panic because she had left a couple of messages and you hadn't called her back. So I gave her your mobile phone number—'

'Well, she hasn't called yet. Where is she?' Star demanded.

'Switzerland...your mother didn't tell me that, but I checked the number after she'd rung off,' Rory admitted.

'Switzerland...what the heck is she doing there?' Star groaned. 'Did you tell her where I was?'

'Yeah...and she got really upset. Then she just hung up again. I'm sorry.' Recognising Star's anxiety, Rory reached for her hand and squeezed it in consolation. 'Do you want that Swiss phone number?'

Star nodded ruefully.

Rory wrote it down and passed it to her. Star dug the piece

of paper into the back pocket of her skirt and wandered very slowly back into the chateau.

Preoccupied as Star had been with concern for her missing mother, she really only noticed how coolly Luc was behaving towards her once the jet had taken off.

'I haven't even asked where we're going,' she muttered guiltily.

'Corsica...'

'Oh, I haven't been there...well, I haven't been *most* places!' she adjusted.

His lean, strong face empty of even a pretence of fleeting amusement, Luc rose to his feet. '*Excuses-moi, mais*...I have work to do,' he drawled glacially.

A heart-stopping vision of French masculine elegance in an unstructured lightweight suit in palest grey, Luc strode off to vanish into the office area of the jet. *Cool?* Luc was acting like the beginning of a new Ice Age. Confused, Star sat on a moment or two before following him. Longing for the light-hearted mood he had been in earlier that day, she perched on the arm of the seat across the aisle from him.

'I appreciate that I've been a bit of a drag since Rory visited—'

Luc kept his attention on the screen of his laptop, but his bold profile hardened.

'I've been worrying about Mum,' she confided.

For a split second a pained light flashed in Luc's narrowed gaze. She wasn't just a poor liar: she was a hopeless one. Having lit up with pure joy at one glimpse of Rory Martin, Star had sunk into silent misery the instant her former lover had departed in his boy-toy car. *Friendship?* All right, so he himself had never had time for close friends, but who did she think she was kidding? She couldn't act for peanuts either. If swarming all over that skinny little twerp in his girly jeans was her idea of friendship, she would be very lonely in the friendship stakes in the future, Luc promised himself wrathfully.

Star cleared her throat awkwardly.

Luc still couldn't bring himself to look at her.

'Juno called Rory from Switzerland and I tried the number, but it was a guesthouse and she'd already moved on without leaving an address,' Star volunteered tautly. 'I know you think she's a...a foolish woman at best and a schemer at worst, but I love her and naturally I'm concerned about her.'

'Naturally,' Luc echoed flatly. 'But to be frank...your mother has a healthy survival instinct. If she's in Switzerland, she must have a good reason for being there.'

'I can't think of any connection, except that that's where she fell pregnant with me,' Star confided.

Luc hadn't known that, but he kept his attention rigidly on the screen.

'You just want me to run along and play...don't you?' Star gathered tightly as the silence stretched.

'*Vraiment!*' Luc flung his arrogant dark head back and subjected her to a sizzling and derisive appraisal. 'After the performance you put on with Rory this afternoon, what more do you expect?'

Her throat caught as she recognised his anger. 'Performance?'

'I have no wish to discuss it further,' Luc ground out harshly.

Star contemplated his rigid profile and it was as if an alarm bell went off inside her head. 'You were jealous...' she whispered, in the tone of one making a fascinating discovery.

Luc slammed his laptop shut with such force it bounced on the desk. He sprang upright. Scorching dark eyes assailed hers in a look of rebuttal as physical as an assault. '*Zut alors!* What do you think I am? An adolescent? I found the sight of *my* wife being so familiar with another man very offensive! That is not jealousy.'

He was so much taller than she was that it took courage

not to be intimidated. But Star was now angry too. Rising to her feet, she squared her slight shoulders. 'Whatever you say…but when you're annoyed with me, you'd better learn to face me with it. I won't put up with the deep-freeze treatment. And by the way, if you saw anything offensive in my behaviour with Rory, it was in your own mind.'

'You flaunted your intimacy with him,' Luc condemned fiercely.

'I've never been intimate with him…not intimate in the way *you* mean!' Star returned tartly, infuriated with him. 'And, since you're *not* jealous…I wonder how it was that you *imagined* you saw sexual intimacy where it has never existed!'

Luc froze, shimmering dark eyes suddenly welding to her flushed face. 'Never…?'

Turning on her heel, Star utilised the words he had used with her only a minute earlier. 'I have no wish to discuss it further.'

A lean hand closed over her shoulder to stay her. *'Star—'*

Star pulled away. 'No! I'm really annoyed with you. Why can't you just admit that you have normal human emotions like everybody else? Instead you tried to put me down as if I'd done something wrong! That's what I can't forgive.'

Leaving silence in her wake, Star returned to the twins, happily dozing in their seats like twin angels. Well, their father is no angel, she thought furiously.

CHAPTER NINE

A HELICOPTER took them the last brief leg of the journey.

'That's the villa down there!' Luc shouted above the noise of the rotors.

Star gazed down into a breathtakingly beautiful wooded gorge and saw a villa with a terracotta roof perched just above a stretch of golden sand. A ribbon of road ran down through steep, tortuous bends beneath the trees, but she could see no other houses. A private hideaway...just when she wanted crowds to prevent her lunging for Luc's jugular vein!

Although Star had a quick temper, she usually cooled down again even quicker. But this time she just found herself getting even angrier with Luc. Luc, whom she had once worshipped rather like a god, whom she had unquestioningly accepted was in every way superior to her humble self. Cleverer, stronger, better than her in every way. But Luc had attacked her once too often with her supposed flaws and mistakes.

Descending from the helicopter, clutching Venus, Star studied the rambling, spacious villa. Backed by a grove of tall cypress and beech trees, the weathered tawny stone gleamed like gold in the glowing light of sunset. Even a sourpuss would have been forced to admit that it was an absolutely out-of-this-world setting. And when Luc showed her through the front door it just got better and better. Marble-tiled floors, stylish, comfortable furniture, ornate lamps and vases, beautiful bedrooms and bathrooms, and cots dressed with broderie anglaise bedding awaiting the twins.

'How did you get this place at such short notice...a cancellation?' she heard herself ask, although she had been assiduously ignoring him.

150

'It's been in the family for a while.'

Star's face took on a jaundiced look. She should have known. Private, exclusive, possessed of every conceivable luxury. 'Was that a Jacuzzi out front?'

'*Oui...*'

'Well, you needn't think you're getting me into that.'

She listened to him audibly exhale, and busied herself with Venus and Mars. She had readied them for bed before they'd left the jet and they were snug in their respective Babygros.

Luc hovered. 'You're not going to have to cook or anything—'

'Oh, I *know* that. You wouldn't want to be poisoned, would you?'

Ignoring that comment, Luc mentioned the maid who would be coming in twice a day, and who would also be available to stay over if they wanted to dine out.

Star put the twins in the cots and thought what truly wonderful babies they were, neither of them one bit bothered by all the different places they had had to sleep recently.

'If you give me the chance, I'll apologise,' Luc drawled levelly.

'Forget it...it would be wasted on me. I'm just sick and tired of you always criticising me—'

'Star...I very much want this to be a special time for us,' Luc said. 'I accept that I spoilt things, but it's not like you to hold spite.'

'No, more's the pity.' Star surveyed him, aquamarine eyes shimmering. It annoyed her right then that he looked so absolutely gorgeous and so absolutely reasonable, as if he was trying to deal gently with a very sulky child. 'I mean, you didn't hang back when it came to censuring my actions, did you? So why did I? And I *did* hold back!'

'If you've got something to say, say it...'

'Have you a pen?'

His black brows pleating, he tugged a gold pen from his inside pocket. Star strolled into the main reception room and espied a notepad by the phone. Sitting down on a sofa, she proceeded to write.

'What are you doing?'

'You're clever when you argue. I want to be sure I'm not knocked off track. I want to be sure I get *everything* out!'

'I think I'll go for a walk on the beach, and maybe by the time—'

'By the time you get back, I'll have cooled off?' Star loosed a driven laugh. 'No chance, Luc. Right, are you ready?'

'Is this really necessary?'

'If you want me to stay married to you beyond the next five minutes, it is very necessary,' Star stated tightly. 'Point one. I do not like being treated like a child. I'm a woman and a mother. I will not be patronised.'

'*D'accord*...OK,' Luc murmured with amusement brightening his eyes.

Star was determined to knock that indulgent look off his darkly handsome face. 'Point two: that winter I fell in love with you, you encouraged me at every turn by not rejecting me. I think you got a kick out of my loving you.'

She had got her wish. His amusement had gone. '*Vraiment*—'

'No, I'm doing the talking here, and then I'm going to bed alone and you are going to *think* about what I've said.'

Luc spread his lean hands wide in an exasperated gesture and strode over to the window.

Star breathed in deep again. 'All that winter, you fed me confusing signals, both before *and* after we were married. You could have shot me down in flames when I said I loved you. If you held back the first time out of pity, it still gave you no excuse to allow me to dog your footsteps, absolutely out of my head with adoration *after* that day.'

Luc swung round, brilliant eyes glinting. 'I didn't want to hurt you.'

'Don't you understand what I'm trying to get you to work

out for yourself?' Star launched at him in frustration. '*Why* did you put up with me? You are not a tolerant, patient guy, and I invaded your space every chance I got. By rights, you should have loathed the sight of me!'

A dark line of colour now demarcated his hard cheek-bones. He said nothing.

Star shook her bright head slowly. 'I mean, just over a week ago I listened to you accuse me of forcing you into situations you didn't want...like you're such a wimpy personality, like you were just totally helpless in the designing paws of a little teenager. You, Luc Sarrazin, chairman of the Sarrazin bank, the guy with the cold, ruthless reputation who doesn't let *anyone* put one over on him!'

'I felt guilty about you...' Luc imparted grimly. 'Whose fault was it that as a child you ended up living with a woman who was a stranger and attending a boarding school? I assumed that my parents would have enough compassion to allow you to stay with us at Chateau Fontaine. As you have cause to know, that was a very stupid and naive assumption.'

'What else could you have done with me? *That* wasn't your fault.'

'I could have tried to help you and your mother. I judged her very harshly on the strength of an hour's meeting.'

'Luc, you were only twenty, and we weren't your responsibility. I was your father's responsibility, and he didn't want to be bothered with me.'

'But I was so angry at the way things turned out that I took nothing further to do with you.'

'You were a little too young to be a father figure...' Star was troubled and frustrated by the direction the dialogue had gone in. But she now saw that Luc had been much more disturbed by events that had effectively been out of his control than she had ever appreciated.

'At the very least I should have visited you—'

'If I made you feel so guilty...I'm glad you stayed away,' Star said woodenly, realising that he had given her another slant on his past behaviour, and really *not* a slant she had had any desire to see. Guilt—a powerful reason to have been unusually tolerant that winter she had fallen in love with him.

'What else is on your list?'

G for Gabrielle. She'd planned to ask him why he hadn't simply told her that he had a woman in his life. With no clear evidence of Luc having an ongoing relationship with Gabrielle, Star had soon dismissed Emilie's confidences about the other woman as being out of date. So it had been a much greater shock to discover on their wedding night that Gabrielle had still been very much a current interest in Luc's life.

'Star...you are sitting there seething,' Luc noted drily.

'I should've gagged you before I commenced attack.' Star emitted a shaken laugh, her triangular face very pale as the point of what he had already told her began to sink in even more deeply and fill her with unbelievable pain. 'I did intend to ask why you went to the extraordinary length of marrying me when you could have just cornered my mother and cleared up the misunderstanding...but you've answered that too. Guilt. Guilt covers everything you ever did, doesn't it? Past, present *and* future.'

Having perceptibly relaxed as her anger visibly waned, Luc now took a hasty step closer. 'What are you trying to say?'

Eyes shuttered, Star stood up, every movement stiff. 'That I've got no plans to forever figure in your mind as that poor deprived child you thought you were rescuing from Mexico. And it's obvious that's all I'm ever going to be. Did you honestly think I'd want to stay around after hearing *that*?'

As she attempted to move past him, Luc shot out a powerful hand to prevent her. 'You misunderstood me...' he gritted.

'No, I asked for the truth and you told me the truth,' Star recited shakily, tiny tremors of reaction starting to ripple through her slender length. 'If it wasn't for the sex, you

wouldn't have any use at all for me. It's about the only thing
I've got to offer, isn't it?'

Luc closed his hand over her rigid shoulder and spun her
round. '*Mais c'est insensé!*... That's crazy!' he launched
down at her roughly. 'Why are you talking like this?'

Star focused on the top button of his aqua silk open-necked
shirt. Inside herself she felt as if she was dying. 'You really
weren't jealous of Rory,' she gasped strickenly. 'My fertile
imagination at fault again! But let me tell you one last thing,
Luc Sarrazin...you can take your over-developed conscience,
your pious outlook and your cruel, unfeeling brain and take
a running jump, because I want nothing more to do with you
in this lifetime!'

Luc seemed stunned into paralysis by that concluding
speech. Star took advantage of his loosened hold to drag
herself free and race for the sanctuary of one of the bedrooms.

Crisis. *Serious crisis.* Those two words stood out in Luc's
head in letters ten feet tall, but he found that for several
deeply disturbing minutes, he couldn't think round them,
over them or under them. Then, for a fleeting moment, he
recalled the sense of self-satisfaction he had experienced in
parrying her questions without even having to think about
them. Now he was in shock at the results. He had hurt her,
really hurt her.

And you were planning to make her fall in love with you
again. A ragged laugh was wrenched from him. The truth
was he hadn't a clue where to start. Total meltdown failure
now stared him in the face. But the only face Luc could see
was Star's...ashen, empty, defeated. As if she had given up
on him finally and for ever. Luc endured another terrifying
few minutes when he couldn't string two simple thoughts
together. He recognised his own instinctive fear for the first
time and headed straight for the drinks cabinet, only to
freeze. Only a wimpy personality needed alcohol to work out

problems…and he hadn't done so well working them out the last time, had he?

The muslin drapes at the window fluttered softly in the light breeze coming in off the Mediterranean. From her bed, Star was watching the sun sink down below the horizon in a crimson blaze of splendour and listening to the soft rush of the surf.

There had been no tears; she felt totally hollow. It was the end, the literal end. Luc's every response eighteen months ago had been prompted by guilt and compassion. She had done all the running; she had *always* done all the running with Luc. Now she was facing the consequences—just as much as he was, she affixed, with a guilt that made her feel even more wretched. Two innocent children were involved now.

As the bedroom door opened, she was jerked out of her reverie. Moonlight glimmered over the paleness of Luc's shirt. Highwire tension was etched in his taut stance just one step inside the door.

'You're right,' he drawled with staggering abruptness, his accent thick as molasses. 'I was jealous of Rory…I was so jealous I felt physically sick. You were ecstatic to see him and you touched him. *Pour l'amour du ciel*…I wanted to beat him up and throw him in the moat!'

Stunned by that blunt confession coming straight at her without warning, Star mumbled. 'Oh…'

'But I did not recognise that I was jealous at the time…' Luc thrust driven fingers through his tousled black hair. 'I thought it was your over-familiarity with him that was making me angry, but when I think back, you might not have done anything I *liked* with him, but then neither did you do anything wrong.'

Star nodded very carefully, as if she was willing him to continue.

Luc moved his hands in an odd jerky motion and then

lunged back against the door, to slam it in a clear burst of
frustration. He thrust his dark head back, hands coiled into
fists. 'I am very, very possessive of you. I know that's not
right, but that seems to be the way I am...'

He sounded really ashamed of that admission. Suddenly
needing to see him better than moonlight allowed, Star sat
up to switch on the bedside lamp. She collided with stagger-
ingly defensive dark eyes, and her heart ached for him as if
he had squeezed it.

'I was very relieved to realise that you and Rory had never
been lovers. But that wasn't right either...'

That this was the guy who had told her to go off and
experiment with boys her own age was silently acknowledged by the self-derisive twist of his wide, sensual mouth.

'So you've got a dog-in-the-manger side to you,' Star muttered tautly.

'I haven't thought about that...' A flash of dismay showed
distinctly in his serious gaze, and even in that tense atmosphere she almost smiled. He looked slightly panicky, as if
she had moved off his authorised script and he wasn't
equipped to handle it.

'What else have you thought about?' she asked thickly.

'That I interpreted certain events in the manner that suited
my view of myself best,' Luc admitted. 'I think I married
you because I knew that sooner or later I would lose control
and end up in bed with you.'

'But, Luc, when you got me, you didn't want me. I was
your wife for six weeks—'

'And I said at the outset it *wasn't* to be a real marriage.
I'm stubborn,' he grated with sudden impatience. 'If I slept
with you, then it was a real marriage, a serious commitment...a commitment I hadn't even considered making at
that stage of my life.'

'So you thought, If I sleep with her, I'll be stuck with
her...and that was enough to keep me in a bed at the foot of

the corridor,' Star said with flat bitterness. 'Thanks for clarifying that.'

'It was for your sake as much my own. And will you for once acknowledge that that entire six weeks was spent waiting for my father to die…and then burying him?' Luc demanded starkly. 'I know you think I'm unfeeling and cold, but I had a lot more on my mind than my own physical needs!'

Hot, shamed colour washed up over Star's startled face. She lowered her head, unable to comprehend how she could possibly have overlooked that harsh background to those weeks for so long. But then she hadn't loved Roland Sarrazin. He had been a distant stranger to her, a grudging guardian, a man with precious little interest in her. 'Yes…'

'I was under a lot of stress, and you were very appealing, but I didn't want to use you just for…comfort,' he bit out very, very low.

At that, Star lifted her head, aquamarine eyes swimming with tears. 'So you used Gabrielle Joly instead…'

Luc studied her in complete shock.

'Yes…I knew about Gabrielle,' Star confirmed, recognising that that really was a surprise to him.

Striding over to the bed, Luc sank down beside her. 'How did you find out about Gabrielle?' he demanded thickly.

She ignored that question. 'I thought you were finished with her…until our wedding night, when I heard you on the phone to her,' she shared chokily.

Luc lifted his hand and pushed her tumbled hair off her cheekbone, stunning dark eyes full of regret but also considerable bemusement. 'And yet you said nothing…you, who could talk up a storm over a leaf falling, said nothing about something so much more important?'

'You spent our wedding night with her.'

'Don't be stupid…' Luc groaned. 'How could you be *that* stupid?'

'I heard you say you were coming over—'

'To return my set of keys to her house…' Unsurprised, it seemed, by Star's incredulous frown, Luc expelled his breath in a hiss of annoyance. 'That's all the excuse I've got. It was crazy…and she was certainly very surprised to see me on that particular night. But that night I just needed to get *out* and I seized the first flimsy excuse I could come up with and acted on it.'

'To return *keys*?' Star repeated in disbelief. 'On our wedding night? You didn't come home that night…do you think I don't know that?'

'I fell asleep in the car by the riverbank…I never entered her home. I dropped off the keys and realised how open to misinterpretation my call was,' he shared with palpable discomfiture. 'I left again immediately.'

Fell asleep in the car? Luc, within a quarter-mile of a home possessed of thirty-odd bedrooms? Luc dropping off keys that he could have had returned without going anywhere near Gabrielle? It was so unlikely a story that Star simply stared at him wide-eyed.

Dark colour overlaid his fabulous cheekbones. 'It was a mad impulse, foolishly acted on because I didn't trust myself within reach of you that night. I knew you would come to me…'

Star dropped her head. He wasn't wrong about that. That had been exactly what she'd planned to do. But eavesdropping on that call had blown her intentions out of the water and left her high and dry, not to mention paralysed with shock, violent jealousy and very real distress.

'And I wasn't sure I had enough will-power to resist such an invitation. I was *burning* for you that night…possibly even a duck T-shirt wouldn't have held me back.'

'I'd bought a really naff black slinky nightie. It was too big for me. I dumped it.'

'I cannot believe that you said nothing after listening in on that call I made to Gabrielle…' Luc framed her face, forcing her to meet his fiercely enquiring gaze.

'What *right* had I to say anything?' Star demanded shakily. 'You had stated up-front that we weren't going to have a normal marriage...and there you were acting on it. That's how it seemed to me. You were just going to go on with your life like I wasn't there, and if I forced the issue, what would I get out of it?'

'The truth?' Luc prompted hoarsely.

'But I couldn't stop you sleeping with her if you wanted to...' Star reeled off brokenly, still bewildered by the idea that an episode which had caused her so much anguish might never actually have happened in reality. 'You could just have told me that what you did with *her* was none of my business. And once I'd pushed you to the stage of saying something like that, it would have been like something written in stone, and it would have been the end of my hoping to make our marriage a p-proper one!'

Luc felt gutted by the time Star had finished speaking; her pain was still so raw. He clenched his teeth, angry that he had caused her that much pain. She had been too damned scared to confront him about Gabrielle. Like a child unable to cope with unpleasant reality, she had spent the remainder of their marriage pretending to be her usual sunny, cheerful self, and *he* hadn't noticed anything different. But still he could not get his mind around the level of savage insensitivity she had believed him capable of.

'How could you credit that I would spend our wedding night with another woman? What sort of a bastard did you think I was that I would humiliate you like that?' Luc demanded. 'I *knew* how you felt about me. Even if I'd been on fire with lust for some other woman I wouldn't have sunk that low.'

'So instead you slept in your car on the riverbank...like a vagrant in a Ferrari,' Star whispered unsteadily. 'How could you ever think I would have imagined you doing something like that?'

'But now I finally know why you left me and never once

thought of coming back,' Luc conceded in sudden harsh conclusion.

Weary of all the emotions he had put her through, Star let her head flop down on his shoulder, breathing in the achingly familiar scent of his warm skin with a mixture of anguish and tormented hunger. 'You can sleep in here tonight...'

'No...short of you tying me to the bed and raping me. I won't allow you to accuse me again of just using you for sexual release.'

'That night at the castle,' Star reminded him helplessly. 'Stop acting like Mr Noble, Mr High-Minded—'

'I can't explain that night I...I just didn't want to leave you...I could think of nothing else but sex as an excuse. It was all that was *left* after you let me believe that the twins were some other man's.'

His lingering annoyance on that score made her tense. But just as suddenly he hauled her all the way into his arms, devouring dark eyes searching hers. 'Whatever else has changed, you still need me, *mon ange*,' he murmured with unhidden satisfaction.

She went limp against him, but not for long. The fiery demand of his sensual mouth on hers awakened her. And the most consuming impatience seemed to possess both of them. Star helped him to haul his shirt over his head, but was sidetracked when he bared his muscular chest, spreading her palms there, pressing her lips lovingly to every part of him she could reach.

He came down with a groan, struggling to snake his hips free of his trousers while she wrenched at her skirt. But the zip caught, Luc gave it one sharp tug, and when it stayed jammed, he just ripped it apart.

'So I'll buy you another ten,' he muttered feverishly, already engaged in extracting her from her T-shirt and capturing a tautened pink peak with a very vocal male groan of appreciation.

Her excitement was so intense she felt drunk and out of

control, heart racing insanely, every pulse pounding. Her body throbbed with a kind of ecstatic torment of anticipation. He traced the damp heat of her readiness and she twisted and turned, frantic for a more forceful invasion, every sense craving him with shameless, helpless abandon.

'I just want you...I just want you.'

'This is not a very cool start to a honeymoon.' Luc freed her of her last garment with a dexterity that was more driven by desperation than actual skill.

'Honeymoon...? Oh...*oh, please*,' Star moaned, clenching her teeth. 'Talk later?'

'If I'm still alive after this much excitement, *mon ange*.' With a ragged laugh, Luc came down on her and entered her in one powerful thrust. A shuddering groan of pleasure escaped him.

Star wasn't capable of vocalising at that point. The height of her excitement was blinding, silencing, all-consuming. The whole centre of her being was locked into every glorious movement he made. It was like suddenly entering heaven and hoping that heaven was endless. Never before had she experienced such a sense of oneness with Luc; never before had she felt sheer joy rippling through her in concert with the wild high of his possession. An intoxicating combination which sent her spinning into an earth-shattering climax of mindless strength.

He held her so close and tight in the aftermath it was a wonder that she could breathe. In fact she didn't think two adults could ever before have occupied so small a space in so large a bed, and that closeness made her feel so good it brought tears to her eyes. She kissed a loving trail across his shoulder, caressed his damp back.

He held her back about six inches from him, but kept their bodies still intimately entwined. His slashing smile made her heart bang up against her ribs. 'I really *do* get a high from giving you pleasure... I just want to do it again...and again...and...and again,' he teased, punctuating each repetition with tiny provocative and still hungry kisses. 'Rain-check on talking?'

Star studied him with passion-glazed eyes of wonderment, happy, so happy, that if she could have stood being separated from him she might have danced round the room. He hadn't gone to Gabrielle on their wedding night. She decided there and then that he was a god among men; Gabrielle had been incredibly gorgeous, yet Luc had clearly ended that relationship because he was getting married. So, whether he recognised the fact or not, he *had* made a commitment to his teenage bride, Star concluded with a wave of enormous satisfaction.

'You look wonderfully smug,' Luc muttered.

Tact seized a rare hold of her. 'I'm just happy...'

Star opened her eyes and lay sleepily still while a vague memory of Luc assuring her that *he* would see to Venus and Mars slowly surfaced.

For goodness' sake, it was eleven! Luc couldn't possibly have managed the twins on his own! Feeling guilty as hell, Star got up, and, hearing sounds from the lounge area, headed in that direction.

Luc was down on his knees with Venus and Mars propped up against the sofa cushions he had dragged down onto the floor for their benefit.

'Daddy...that's what you call me in English, but if it's French, which you have to learn as well,' he was warning them, 'it is Papa,' he sounded out carefully, and then repeated it, even more slowly.

It was so sweet. The twins made various little sounds like a chorus. Mars was the most earnest in his efforts to acquire this knew knowledge. Venus clutched at her toes, but she didn't take her attention from her father's darkly handsome visage for a second. Star had never seen her daughter stay that still in one place for so long.

'Luc...how the heck did you cope?'

His dark head turned, his eyes gleaming with amusement. 'It was a true learning experience... *Zut alors!* They have some appetite for their breakfast! I forgot to arrange high chairs, so feeding them was difficult, but we managed, and I got them washed and dressed as well,' he pointed out with considerable pride in his achievement.

The twins were only wearing vests. Star swallowed back laughter. 'You washed them too?'

'Of course I did...with a sponge. Venus turned that into quite a game. Watch Papa try to catch me,' Luc shared with a rueful grin of recollection, rising upright as Star bent down to cuddle their son and daughter. 'She found out that I'm clumsy, but persistent! I now badly need a shower.'

There was a fine dust of what just might have been baby cereal in his black hair. He hadn't managed to shave yet either. He paused in the doorway and looked back at her. 'I have very real respect for you now, *mon ange,*' he asserted seriously. 'How did you cope with them on your own? It was *really* hard work. I felt like I needed another set of eyes and at least two extra pairs of hands.'

'You were brilliant, absolutely brilliant,' she assured him softly, her eyes full of warmth.

'*Non*...I was lousy this time around, but next time I'll be better.'

A lot of other men would have been in a bad mood after more than five hours of childcare, and most rich men would have suggested that perhaps leaving Bertille behind had been a major mistake. But Luc wanted to be a hands-on father, not a distant one, and she was impressed that he wanted to rise to that challenge when he didn't have to.

While Luc was in the shower, Star started getting dressed. Her mobile phone buzzed. Realising it might be her mother calling, she lunged for it like a maniac.

'*Star?*' Juno gasped.

'Yes, it's me. Where on—?'

'I am *so* sorry that you've been forced to go back to Luc.

This is all my fault. I feel so dreadful, but, darling, you don't need to stand one more day of that womanising rat! I'm coming to rescue you...OK?'

'I don't want to be rescued, Mum.'

'But—'

'I still love Luc, and we're together again, and you really must stop talking like he's Public Enemy Number One just because he's Roland Sarrazin's son,' Star spelled out steadily. 'And that wedding night stuff? I was *wrong*. He wasn't with Gabrielle.'

'Surely you don't believe that, just on his say so? It's a good thing I'm flying into France this afternoon!'

Star stiffened in dismay, feeling that the last thing her marriage required right now was her mother's enervating presence, and then feeling instantly guilty at even thinking that. 'But we're not at Chateau Fontaine. Luc and I are on our honeymoon, and although I very much want to see you, and hear your side of what happened with that loan Emilie gave you—'

'Star...I've already sent Emilie a cheque in full repayment of that loan.'

'How on earth have you managed to do that?' Star asked weakly. 'Have you borrowed the money from someone—?'

'When will you be back from this honeymoon?' her mother cut in impatiently.

'In two weeks.'

'Well, if you're prepared to wait another two weeks to meet my new husband, I expect I can wait another two weeks to meet my son-in-law again... Luc's got more lives than a cat with you, hasn't he?'

'Mum...did you say what I think you just said?'

'You're just going to have to wait for the exciting details,' Juno pointed out with satisfaction. 'But I can tell you that I am blissfully happy. So I'll see you in a fortnight and you can meet Bruno then too. Bye, darling!'

Star sank down on the bed in shock while the twins crawled round her feet.

She was still staring into space when Luc emerged from the bathroom, just a towel between him and six foot three inches of immodest but gorgeous display. But for once Star had something to deflect her attention from his devastating presence, and couldn't even raise a smile when at first glimpse of Venus and Mars Luc yanked up a dressing robe and hurriedly pulled it round him.

'What's wrong?' Luc demanded the instant he saw her face.

'Mum phoned. She's gone off and got married to some guy she could only have known about two weeks.' Star gazed at Luc in weary apology, her eyes anxious. 'Well, you know it's sure to end in tears.'

Star went on to add that Juno had sent Emilie a cheque in full repayment of the loan.

'This new husband has money…either that or he's parted with his life savings. Not much we can do about this in the short term. Stop being such a pessimist!' His lean, dark features concerned, Luc tugged her up into his arms. 'Why should it be a disaster?'

Star sighed ruefully and rested her troubled brow against his warm bare chest. The tenderness of her mother's too often broken heart did not bear thinking of. 'Luc, you know as well as I do that maybe one man in a thousand could stand Juno's fits and starts…and to get married so quickly she must've fallen head over heels, and she'll be devastated if this Bruno character lets her down—'

'Bruno…and Juno?' Luc strung the two names together and a slight shudder rippled through his powerful frame. 'Seriously?'

'He sounds like a big thug.'

'*Mon ange*…' Luc pushed up her chin, dark eyes bold and level. 'Whatever happens, we will both support her. It's just a little unfortunate that she hates the sight of me.'

'Mostly because she too thinks you went off to Gabrielle on our wedding night,' Star admitted reluctantly.

Luc dealt her a riveted glance.

'And Emilie thinks that too, which is the only reason why she agreed not to tell you about Venus and Mars being born,' Star added in a craven undertone. 'Now I don't have a *single* secret left that you don't know about…isn't that good?'

Luc had the appearance of a male being torn in two different directions. Between strangling her fast and strangling her slowly. Then a muscle jerked at the corner of his hard, compressed mouth and suddenly he gave vent to a grudging groan of grim appreciation.

'You vented your grief liberally…everywhere with every possible person?'

She nodded apologetically. 'Talking helped.'

'But from now on you have to be discreet…you only allow your feelings to overflow in my direction.'

'Of course,' Star hastened to assure him, very grateful to have got over that last embarrassing revelation without an explosion.

'You talk to me about personal things. *Only* me,' he stressed.

'I get the message,' she swore. 'I'll try—'

'Trying isn't good enough. *J'insiste*,' Luc laid down with awesome authority.

'How much do you know about your real father?' Luc enquired casually that evening as they strolled back to the car after dining at a quayside restaurant in Calvi.

Star glanced up at him in surprise. 'Not much, but he really broke Mum's heart. Even eighteen months ago, when I finally got the chance to ask about him, she dissolved into floods of tears. She met him when she was working as a chalet girl in Gstaad. She was only nineteen. He asked her to marry him while neglecting to admit that he was already engaged,' she shared with a grimace. 'Then his fiancée turned up and Juno fled back to London without ever seeing him again.'

'What was his name?' Luc drawled lazily.

'I never asked...it didn't seem important, not when talking about him was upsetting her so much. He really did mess up her life.' Star sighed. 'Mum was brought up by her grandparents, and when they died she inherited nearly half a million pounds—'

'I never knew that.' Luc lifted her up into the four-wheel drive as if she couldn't possibly manage to clamber up on that big step all on her own. But Star was smiling, revelling in the manner in which Luc had been treating her since their first night in Corsica. As if she was spun glass, and so precious. She just loved it.

'Why should you have done? Phillipe had gambled away the lot by the time I was three years old. Mum only married him because she was pregnant with me, and I expect he was tempted by her inheritance.'

'I'm starting to see why Emilie believes your mother has had more than her fair share of bad luck.'

Delighted by that new tolerance, Star gave him a glowing smile in reward.

Two weeks later, Star lay in Luc's arms at dawn.

She was wide awake. They were flying home in a few hours. Wherever Luc was would be home, she acknowledged with complete contentment. Corsica was where they had grown closer than she had ever dreamt possible. It was a gorgeous island, full of spectacular scenery and forests and picturesque villages. This villa would always be a very special place for them.

Deciding to surprise him with breakfast in bed, she eased out of Luc's embrace. She watched his hand move across the bed, as if he was seeking her, as if he could feel her absence even when he was asleep. He would sleep late. He deserved to, she conceded with a grin, admiring the long sweep of his golden back in the soft light filtering through the curtains. He was a wonderful lover, a fabulous father, and shaping up really well as a soulmate. And last night he had spoken heresy…he was planning to *cut* his working hours and reorganise his schedule so that he travelled less.

Over dinner last night she had shared with him the details of the twins' premature birth and the subsequent months of frantic worry and stress. He had been so shocked. He honestly hadn't realised how at risk Venus and Mars had once been. He wished very much that he had been there to support them all, but he didn't blame her for not contacting him. He accepted that what he had said the morning after their son and daughter's conception had convinced Star that he really wouldn't want to know that he was a father.

I love him, I love him, I love him, Star reflected as she thought of that generous understanding and acceptance which had so relieved her. Perhaps tonight she would tell him that she loved him again. While she waited for the kettle in the kitchen, she lifted a glossy magazine which the maid must have been skimming through the evening before. On the front page she saw Luc's distinctive script. A note he had jotted down? Naturally nosy, she turned it upside down to read what he had written. A name and a date. A name that still had the power to drain Star of oxygen and turn her pale.

It *had* to be an old magazine. Not that that quite wiped out the huge sense of hurt she was experiencing. Naturally it was a smack in the face to appreciate that Gabrielle Joly must also have shared a bed here with Luc at one time. Suddenly all her own memories began feeling soiled. She turned the magazine round, just to check the date of it. Only then did she realise in sick dismay that the spoiling of sentimental memories was the *least* she had to worry about!

The magazine was only two months old, so when Luc had jotted down 'Gabrielle arriving' it had been barely a *month* before Star had come back into his life. Star hugged herself, suddenly chilled to the marrow. How could she now have faith in *anything* Luc had told her about Gabrielle Joly?

Luc had allowed her to believe that Gabrielle had been out of his life for a long time. And yet Gabrielle had still been his mistress as recently as two months ago! Star was shattered. Was Luc planning to keep both a wife and a mistress? What else could she believe? If Gabrielle Joly still held his interest after what Star now estimated to be a relationship of several years' duration, the beautiful blonde had to be very important to him. Far more important than Star had *ever* been prepared to consider...

CHAPTER TEN

STAR was gutted by misery.

She would have to wait until they got back to the chateau to confront Luc with her suspicions; it would be sheer madness to embark on what was likely to be a very distressing scene at the outset of a journey home.

So Luc had to make his own breakfast. He had never had to do that before, and it was not an entirely successful operation. When he tried to kiss Star good morning, he got pushed away and snapped at. By the time they boarded the jet, the atmosphere was explosive. Ignoring Luc's repeated demands to know what was wrong, Star concentrated her attention on Venus and Mars.

Ten minutes into the flight, Luc rose from his seat. 'Look at me, Star—'

'I don't want to look at you right now,' she admitted tightly, and lifted her magazine higher.

Luc snatched it out of her hands with a suddenness that shook her into looking up.

'Stand up,' he told her, dark eyes glittering with anger. 'We'll talk in private.'

'No, I—'

'*D'accord…*' Without warning, Luc simply bent down, scooped her out of her seat and carried her down the plane. 'We are not going to fight in front of the children.'

'Put me down this minute…' she hissed furiously.

Luc dumped her down into another seat and lounged back across the aisle from her.

'We're flying home to a very big party.'

That startling announcement took the wind from Star's angry sails. 'What are you talking about?'

'Being such a romantic guy,' Luc drawled with withering derision, 'I decided to stage the wedding reception we never had as a surprise. Three hundred guests will be waiting to greet us, including your mother and her seriously rich new husband, Bruno Vence. Be warned, Bruno is very small, and he has hair and eyes that are an exact match of yours. And now for the best bit of all. Your wedding dress is waiting for you in the main sleeping compartment.'

'My...my *what*?' Star gasped, already sufficiently thrown by the announcement of the reception and utterly bewildered by the apparent fact that he seemed to know more about Juno's husband than she did.

'You never had the wedding you wanted. Since that was my fault, I have arranged for a church blessing, and this time you get to wear a wedding dress.'

'I can't...I just can't.'

Luc lowered his arrogant dark head. Shimmering dark eyes alight with outrage locked onto hers. 'Oh, yes, you *will*!' he growled. 'You will not embarrass me in front of three hundred people. So ship out, dress up and join the grown-ups. Being in a bad, bad sulky mood is not an excuse for your behaviour since you got up this morning!'

'How about...Gabrielle?' Star whispered raggedly.

Luc stared at her, a pleat forming between his winged ebony brows. 'I don't see the connection.'

'I'll show you...wait a minute.' Star hurried back to her original seat to lift her bag and dig out the magazine cover she had brought from the villa as evidence. Her hands shook. Now the moment had come, she didn't want to confront Luc. Her head was spinning. He had organised these wonderful, wonderful events for her as a surprise, she was now appreciating in shock. They were to have a church blessing and she was to wear a wedding dress and finally be officially introduced to loads of relatives and guests as his wife. And if it hadn't been for the magazine cover she was crumpling between her hands, right now she would have been ecstatically happy.

Luc was poised exactly where she had left him. His darkly handsome face still as glass, he watched her approach. It was a long time since she had seen Luc wear that chilling expression and her skin crawled with foreboding; he had his defences back up. He was guilty; he had to be guilty. He was just waiting to see how much she knew.

In silence, Star extended the magazine cover.

'High drama,' Luc breathed with licking scorn. 'But I don't read this sort of rubbish.'

'It's something you've written on the cover...'

Luc perused his own handwriting. His hard jawline squared. *'So?'*

That undeniably aggressive demand for further clarification wasn't quite the reaction Star had expected. 'Well, it's obvious, isn't it?' she said shakily.

'On the basis of two words and a date I scribbled down the last weekend I spent in Corsica, you decided...what?'

Having to spell it all out somehow made it even more humiliating. A burst of anger pierced the fog of pain and despair which had enveloped Star throughout the morning. 'You're still sleeping with her...you never got rid of her...*all this time* that we've been married, she's continued to be your mistress!' she condemned rawly.

'Are you finished?' Dark eyes as glacial and dangerous as black ice rested on her. 'My relationship with Gabrielle died a natural death several weeks before I even married you! Late last year she got married—'

'Married?' Star stressed in shock.

'During their honeymoon, her husband, Marc, was seriously injured in a road accident. He was only recently released from hospital. When a mutual friend told me of their situation, and of Marc's need for rest and recuperation, I offered them the use of the villa for a holiday.'

Shaken by what he was telling her, Star blinked rapidly. 'But—'

'I haven't seen Gabrielle since she moved to Dijon last year. I was invited to her wedding but was unable to attend.' Luc scanned Star's drawn face with ice-cool eyes.

Star felt awful. 'Luc, I—'

'Gabrielle and I were companions and occasional lovers for a couple of years. It suited both of us. Neither of us wanted to be tied down and we parted just as casually,' Luc informed her grimly. 'I can't understand why you should *still* be so obsessed with her.'

Her face was burning. She could feel the heat of her own severe embarrassment. 'I'm really sorry,' she whispered.

'And I'm really angry with you,' Luc ground out with a newly learned forthrightness which was ironically very unwelcome at that moment.

The thoughts she had thought, the suspicions she had cherished, the very feelings she had gone through over the past hours since reading that stupid note on the magazine now struck Star as rather hysterical.

'For two weeks I've been planning all this behind your back...the church, the dress, the big party...' Luc vented a bitter laugh, a really bleak look in his eyes now, which ripped her to shreds inside. 'And all you've been thinking about all morning is walking out on our marriage again! Tell me, were you looking for a good excuse to leave me?'

White as death now, Star gazed up at him, her tummy flipping with fear. 'It wasn't like that. I got all worked up, and I *was* scared you might still be involved with Gabrielle, but maybe that's because I still feel insecure...Luc, I'm sorry.'

He closed his hands over her slim shoulders in a firm grip. His dark eyes were tough enough to strip paint. 'You are not leaving me again. I don't care if I have to chain you to a wall somewhere...you are *not* leaving me again!' he vented with raw emphasis.

Trembling with reaction, Star watched him stride away. She was deeply shaken by the amount of emotion he had revealed in that last speech. This time around Luc had been so quick, so ready to offer her a commitment to their marriage. But *she* had held back, refusing to give him her trust, making him feel as if he was on trial even though she had denied that. And she loved him so much! So why had she hurt him as she just had with accusations that were patently ridiculous in the light of his behaviour in recent weeks?

Bertille met them at the airport. Enchanted, like Star, when she saw Venus and Mars in the little page boy and bridesmaid outfits Luc had had made up for their children, the young nanny was even more impressed when she saw Star in her wedding gown, wearing a superb Sarrazin diamond tiara in her hair.

'I really *adore* the dress,' Star told Luc in the limo on the way to the church, tracing the beautiful beading sewn into the exquisite fabric. 'How did you pick it?'

'I didn't pick it. I just told the designer that you would want to look like a fairytale princess and, since you're so incredibly talented at embroidery, it had to be of outstanding quality. I only specified that it had to be pure white.'

'You know more about my dreams than I really ever give you credit for,' she acknowledged humbly.

'You'd better read this…' Producing a cutting from a French newspaper, Luc planted it into her hand. 'That's where my information concerning your mother came from. I suppose I should have given it to you yesterday, when I first saw it.'

Still horribly conscious of Luc's distance with her, but feeling she deserved it, Star stared down at the blurry photo of Juno and her male companion. She only then recalled that strange crack Luc had made about the man having her hair and eyes. Bruno Vence was fifty-three years old, described as a Swiss industrialist and a lifelong bachelor. Her mother was described only as an 'old flame'. Obviously the gossip columnist hadn't known her name. But Bruno's friends were supposed to be in severe shock at him racing off to get married to a woman they had never heard of and never met.

'Yesterday…you had this yesterday?' Star frowned, wondering why he hadn't shared it with her sooner.

Luc reached for her hand suddenly, and gripped it very tightly in his, his tension palpable. 'I just have this very strong feeling that Bruno Vence is your father. I met him last year at a business conference. I noticed his eyes were like yours, a very distinctive and unique colour, but I never thought anything of it. *Now* I'm thinking…'

'Luc, what's wrong?'

'Nothing is wrong,' he stated almost aggressively.

'Even if he is my father, and I really do think that's a *very* far-fetched idea,' Star told him gently, 'I won't be upset. Is that what you're worrying about? All I care about is that he should be good to Mum. But, most of all, I don't want anything to spoil this wonderful day.'

'So far it's been a shambles!' Luc groaned.

'No…no, I was very stupid, but nothing's been spoilt for me because I still have you here beside me,' Star swore soothingly, smoothing his tense fingers with her free hand. 'And you are very, very special to me, and so is our marriage. I know now that I want to be with you for ever, Luc, and I'm sorry it took me so long to admit that.'

Luc was very still, and then he released his breath in a sudden hiss. Snapping his arms round her tiny waist, he took her into his arms and kissed her half senseless with an almost desperate passion that just blew her away. He was pleased. She got that message. Probably because he now had the assurance that she was never, ever going to take the children he adored away from him, she reflected, just a little sad that that was the main concern in his mind.

On the steps of the church, with a photographer snapping merrily away, Luc tried to tidy her mussed hair and Star wiped the lipstick off his mouth. It would be pretty obvious to their children some day that a major clinch had occurred on the way to the church.

Heartstoppingly cool, dark and handsome in his formal suit, Luc took her hand and walked her into the little Norman church. The simple blessing that followed recalled for Star her feelings on their wedding day, and by the time they turned from the altar she was feeling full of bridal joy. So intent had she been on the proceedings that she hadn't taken the slightest interest in the fact that the church was packed with guests.

But no sooner did she turn round than her mother appeared in front of her. Comfortably under five feet tall, Juno's youthfully pretty face was wreathed with excitement beneath her cropped blonde curls. 'Star…I have someone here who very much wants to meet you.'

It wasn't the time. It wasn't the place. But then that was Juno, Star acknowledged, feeling Luc's arm tighten round her like an iron band while wondering what on earth was still making her husband so very tense. Surely a church blessing didn't fill a male with the same apprehension as a wedding ceremony?

In her heels, Star was looking eye to eye with the older man who had stepped forward to stand by her mother's side. It was a sharp shock to meet those eyes so like her own, eyes which were unashamedly wet with tears. Bruno Vence shook his greying copper head in mute acknowledgement of his strong emotion before he reached out gratefully to grasp Star's instinctively extended hands.

'I believe you already know who I am…' Her father breathed unevenly.

Five minutes later, in a whirl of confusion, Star found herself sitting in an unfamiliar stretch limousine with Juno and Bruno, not to mention Venus and Mars strapped into conveniently waiting car seats. However, the gathering mysteriously lacked Luc. Star frowned. 'Where's Luc?'

'We can drive straight to the airport and both you and the children will be whisked onto my yacht and out of French territory before anyone can do anything to stop us,' Bruno Vence informed her with impassive calm. 'Your mother believes that your husband must've blackmailed you into agreeing to return to him and that he has used custody of your children as a threat over you.'

'Are you trying to kidnap me?' Star exclaimed in incredulous horror, quite impervious to the fact that Luc had both threatened and blackmailed her at one stage, as he was now entirely forgiven for those sins. 'Juno, how could you *do* this to me? I want Luc...I want my husband!'

'Are you satisfied now, my love?' Bruno Vence asked her anxious mother with a wry smile. 'You see, Star loves Luc. I told you that it looked that way in the church. Our grandchildren are very fortunate to have loving parents.'

'But I wanted to take her and the children away with us,' Juno confided tearfully.

'I'd like to take my daughter away too, so that I could get to know her better,' Bruno murmured with a rueful glance at Star's frowning face. 'But she's an adult now, with a life of her own, and it would be very much simpler if we just made regular visits.'

Star's tension evaporated. 'You gave me quite a fright...'

'Your mother must accept that you are happy in your marriage,' he pointed out apologetically. 'In-laws who are troublemakers are rarely welcome.'

Star leant forward and kissed his cheek without hesitation. 'I think I'll be very happy to get to know you as a father.' She then shifted over beside her disappointed mother and hugged her tight in consolation. 'Now I'd like to hear about your marriage, and don't you dare skip a single detail!' she warned.

Twenty-one years earlier, in Gstaad, Juno had been confronted—*not* by Bruno's fiancée, as the woman had claimed, but by a possessive ex-girlfriend.

'I tried very hard to trace Juno in London,' Bruno shared heavily, holding her mother's hand in his. 'But I failed, because within a couple of months of leaving Gstaad she had impulsively married Phillip Roussel and gone abroad with him.'

'I've always known where Bruno was, but I just assumed he was a married man. Then, the day I had to give up the art gallery, I read a piece in a gossip column that mentioned he was single.' Juno blushed and lowered her lashes. 'But I really only flew out to ask him for a loan, because I was so upset and ashamed at getting Emilie into such a pickle.'

Star immediately knew that the only thing on Juno's mind on that flight to Switzerland had been seeing Bruno again, and she hid a smile.

Bruno was surveying his wife with immense pride and pleasure. 'When your mother walked into my office, I was transfixed. Juno was and is the love of my life. I want you to know that, Star.'

'Your father proposed over lunch an hour later,' Juno proffered. 'It was so romantic, and, you know, twenty years ago he said he *wasn't* a romantic man—but he just couldn't wait to get me to the altar!'

Bruno reddened.

When Star stepped out of the limousine at Chateau Fontaine, Luc was standing on the bridge, seemingly deaf and blind to the greetings of arriving guests.

'We'll see to the children...' Juno called after Star.

For once, the twins were not first in Star's mind. She threaded her passage through the sea of parked cars and headed like a homing pigeon for Luc. The instant he saw her he strode forward, impervious to all onlookers, and pulled her straight into his arms. 'Where the *hell* have you been?' he breathed raggedly. 'And don't you dare tell me you've only come home to pack!'

'No, I'm staying until I'm a skeleton in the family vault.'

'Not funny,' Luc growled, his dark drawl quivering.

'I got to know my father a little. Nice guy, but tough—perfect for Mum. Knows her inside out, adores her, can't believe his luck...they're like a couple of teenagers,' she shared breathlessly.

Luc possessed himself of her hand. 'You won't believe what I was thinking,' he muttered tautly. 'When you and the twins suddenly vanished into that bloody big limo, I suddenly thought I was never going to see you again. I *know* how your mother feels about me—'

'Luc...' A female voice interposed uncertainly.

Luc swung round and then lowered his gaze to focus on his tiny mother-in-law. He froze.

'If Star says you didn't carry on with that Gabrielle on your wedding night, that's good enough for me.'

'We agreed you weren't going to say that,' Bruno groaned from behind Juno.

'But Luc needs to know that I don't believe that any more, and that I intend to like him from now on!' Juno argued.

'Thank you, Juno,' Luc murmured hurriedly.

Her mother gave him a big hug and almost squashed Venus in the process. Hovering in the background, Bertille offered her assistance.

Cradling Mars in one arm, Bruno smiled and extended his other hand to Luc. 'I'm sure you appreciate my daughter.'

'Even *more* since you brought her home,' Luc completed levelly.

Minutes later, Luc closed an arm back round Star. 'You look totally ravishing and gorgeous in that dress, *mon ange*.'

Her heartbeat quickened as she collided with his eyes and she just smiled and smiled.

While drinks were being served, Luc introduced her to loads of people. Star saw Emilie in the crush, but didn't get the opportunity to do more than exchange a brief hug and the promise of conversation at some later stage. A wonderful buffet meal awaited them, delightfully informal and unfussy, just as Star preferred things. Luc stayed by her side all the time. In fact he was like superglue, and her mother had to be quite pushy to manage to share a private word with her.

'I just want to say that I'm sorry that I browbeat Bruno into spiriting you and the twins away from Luc at the church,' Juno confided then worriedly. 'When I saw how distraught Luc was when we brought you back, I was really very ashamed. I never thought he had it in him to really love you as he so obviously does.'

Well, he loves the kids certainly, Star conceded inwardly, too used to her mother's love of exaggeration to credit that viewpoint. As Emilie waved at her, Star passed on from her mother to settle down on a seat beside the older woman.

'I'm overjoyed to see Luc and you together like this,' Emilie told her warmly.

'By the way, that wedding night thingy I thought happened with Gabrielle...' Star whispered urgently. 'I misjudged Luc. It never happened.'

'I'm relieved to hear that, because I always did find it rather difficult to believe,' the older woman admitted gently. 'At the same time, I was very much to blame for what happened between you and Luc that winter.'

Star gave Emilie an amazed look. 'What on earth are you saying?'

Emilie sighed. 'I tried to be a matchmaker and I encouraged you to love Luc. But you were far too young, and Luc was too upset by Roland's illness to concentrate on his own feelings. I should have waited at least another year. I'm a terrible old plotter and planner, Star.'

'No, you're not,' Star told her.

'The main reason I gave Juno all that money was...oh, this is dreadful to have to confess,' the older woman whispered guiltily. 'Star, I *knew* there was a fair chance that the art gallery would fail, and I was praying that if it did it would bring you and Luc and the children together. You have no idea how wretched he was after you left him.'

Star's ears pricked up. Shaken though she was at what

Emilie had revealed, her reference to Luc being wretched superceded all other things. 'Wretched?'

'And not being able to tell him where you were seemed so cruel, but I had given you my promise and you had been badly hurt. However, Luc was dreadfully unhappy as well.'

'Was he? He was worried, of course. I was very childish, not getting back in touch—'

'Star…' Luc intervened from several feet away. 'We get to open the dancing with a waltz.'

'Dancing too?' Star gasped, jumping up and then freezing. 'How do you waltz?'

'You can pick it up.'

'In front of three hundred people?' she yelped. 'Can you jive?'

'No—'

'Fancy picking that up in front of three hundred people?'

'You do have a way of making a point, *ma femme*.' Luc framed her face and kissed her softly, tenderly on her surprised lips. 'I want everybody to go home so that I can be alone with you.'

'Party pooper,' she teased, a shiver of such powerful physical awareness gripping her she blushed. 'OK…I'll try to waltz, but we go slow.'

They drifted round the magnificent ballroom, so enveloped in each other that Star never even noticed what her feet were doing. And when they finally came off the floor, a long while later, Rory appeared with an attractive blonde by his side and apologised for his late arrival. Star was really delighted that Luc had thought to invite him.

Late evening, with only family members remaining, Star and Luc went upstairs. She snuggled up against him and whispered happily and without even thinking about it, 'I *still* love you so much…'

Luc stopped dead outside their bedroom door. 'No, you don't,' he countered. 'I'm still working on that.'

'What are you talking about?' she demanded.

A faint furrow drew his ebony brows together. 'You said *still*...are you saying you never stopped loving me?'

'Didn't I tell you I was going to love you all my life?'

'But then you ran away,' Luc pointed out flatly. 'Stayed away. I had to make threats to get you back, and you didn't exactly grab at the chance to stay married to me—not that I can blame you for that, but—'

'Oh, Luc, I have done a number on you...' Star said guiltily as she opened the bedroom door, thinking that the corridor wasn't the best place to be staging such a personal dialogue. 'I was just trying to be cautious for both our sakes, and I was scared of being hurt again.'

'I don't need to hear you saying you love me again until you can *really* mean it...'

'I mean it now.'

'But how can you?' His dark eyes were very strained. 'I messed up everything eighteen months ago. I didn't even know what was going on in my *own* mind, never mind yours! I drove you away. If I had set out to make a hash of our marriage I couldn't have done better than I have done so far.'

'But you're doing just great...' Star protested.

'I have been trying,' Luc acknowledged—rather touchingly, she felt. 'I took your love for granted when I had it. I liked having you loving me. You were spot-on when you said that. But even when you had gone, and I was bloody miserable, I still didn't grasp *why*! I just thought I was worried about you.'

'I'm here now, and I still love you very, very much,' Star repeated soothingly.

'I had this nightmare last night...and that's how I realised...*finally*...that I love you,' Luc delivered jerkily, a dark rise of colour highlighting his cheekbones.

Star was a little confused. 'A nightmare?'

Luc shrugged, studied his feet. 'It was stupid. I dreamt that Bruno and Juno would take you away. Juno never took to me, so there was no reason why *he* should—and, believe me, if your father wanted you to vanish, he's got the power to do it. It made me feel…sick, knowing that—'

'Oh, Luc.' Star sighed painfully, decided never, ever to tell him that there had been the smallest risk or chance of her vanishing in case he hated her mother for ever.

'So when you got into their car outside the church…and then I saw that the twins were gone too…that's the moment I registered that I loved you…when I thought I had lost the lot of you—my whole family!' he grated, lifting his arrogant dark head and studying her with such powerful emotion that her heart tipped over inside her. 'And I hadn't even *told* you how I felt.'

'Are you sure it wasn't just panic?'

Luc loosed a reluctant laugh at that question. Casting off his jacket, he closed his arms slowly round her. 'I've been in love with you for a very long time—'

'You can tell me anything,' Star encouraged.

He swept her onto the bed and pulled her close. 'First, I lost interest in Gabrielle. Then I just liked you…you fascinated me, and I suppose that's where I should have grasped that I was feeling something I'd never felt before. But I *didn't* grasp it. You have no idea how devastated I was when you left me. It was like the light went out of my life. So I just blamed you for making me feel that bad.'

'Typical…' she said, softly kissing the corner of his beautiful mouth, cherishing that phrase about her being a 'light'.

'And everything with you was *always* devastating.'

'The enemy tank syndrome?'

'Thinking the kids were some other man's, thinking I'd lost your love, not even knowing why I wanted you to still love me and then feeling really bitter—'

'I told you love was messy.'

'Then I seized on the twins as an excuse to hang onto you, so I didn't have to work out how I really felt.' Star removed his tie and began unbuttoning his shirt.

'I'm never going to say all this again,' Luc warned her very seriously, and she smiled against his warm, muscular chest, knowing she would plague the life out of him for any tiny detail he overlooked.

'I planned to make you fall in love with me again,' he explained.

'Nothing like not noticing what you've already got. So that's why I qualified for the honeymoon,' she gathered with amusement.

'I got the honeymoon too, and it felt incredibly self-indulgent,' Luc confided, and lifted her head to steal a passionate kiss. And things just got out of hand, much the way they usually did when they got that close. It was quite a while before they got talking again and, they were sealed together like twin magnets when they did.

'I thought you'd got over me and fallen for Rory,' Luc relived with a shudder of still sensitised recollection. 'I felt threatened, which is why I laid in with all the threats about going to court over the twins.'

'It was a loving friendship, Luc.'

Brilliant dark eyes assailed hers. 'Now you are really and truly and for ever married to me, you're not allowed loving friendships with other men. In all the time we were separated there wasn't *one* other woman in my life.'

'Seriously?' A sudden delighted smile curved her lips, and then she laughed with no tact whatsoever. 'No wonder you wanted one last night with me…oh, Luc, there wasn't anyone else for me either!'

'But you were thinking about it with Rory.'

Star gave him a loving look, recognising in that raw edge to his dark drawl that he was sometimes too clever for his own good. 'I honestly didn't think you wanted me or cared about me at all—'

'I adore you, and I am never letting you go,' Luc swore, with all the fervour a woman in love could ever have wished to receive. 'It took me a very long time to get there, but now

that I have I know exactly what I want most out of life and
that is you.'

Star heaved an ecstatic sigh.

'I just wish I hadn't missed out on you being pregnant...'
Luc admitted ruefully.

'You missed nothing. I was like a small balloon.'

'You *couldn't* look like a small balloon.'

'Just you wait and see—'

'You mean you'd consider extending the family again?'
Luc tensed. 'Are you sure it would be safe for you?'

'Don't be silly.' Star smiled at his concern. 'Since you're
such a great father, your talents should be fully stretched, so
I will definitely think about having another baby some time.'

'We'll talk it over with a doctor first,' Luc asserted with
natural caution.

Just ten months later, Star became a mother again. Being
Star, she hadn't planned the event, but was incredibly pleased
and excited when she found out. Luc spent most of her pregnancy worrying and made her consult several doctors. Star
only worried about Luc and enjoyed a perfectly healthy,
happy nine months. She give birth to another little boy.

At the chirstening, Bruno admitted covertly to Luc that he
was rather grateful they had not taken Juno up on her suggestion that this latest grandson be called Moon. Star's
mother lamented that men were so old-fashioned about
names and sighed to hear Venus now being called Vivi for
short. She was really very shocked when Luc named his second son Orion, and Star's father just burst out laughing.

After putting Vivi and Mars, who were now lively tod-
dlers, to bed that same evening, Star and Luc couldn't resist
looking in again at Orion, snuggled in his four-poster cot like
a little prince.

'Our genes mingled this time.' Star sighed with satisfaction, for their youngest son had Luc's dark hair and her eyes.
'It's like a sign, isn't it?'

Luc laughed and folded her into his arms. 'I don't need a sign to know that I am very, very happy with you.'

'I know. You were shaping up to be a pretty miserable guy before I came along.' Star gazed up into his stunning dark eyes and felt gloriously dizzy.

'I love you...' he murmured softly.

She curved even closer, reasoning that she needed the support, and whispered the same words back in between kisses. It was a long time before they made it down to dinner that evening.

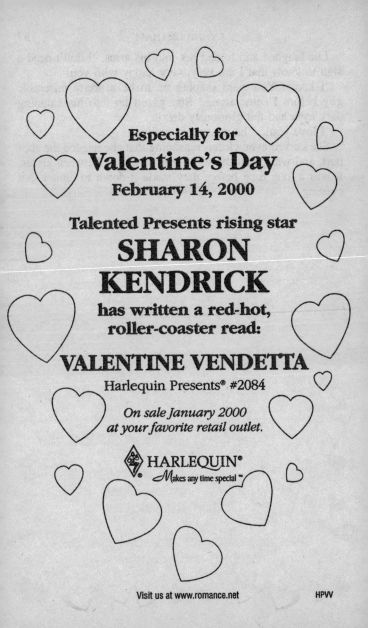

London's streets aren't just paved with gold—they're home to three of the world's most eligible bachelors!

You can meet these gorgeous men, and the women who steal their hearts, in:

NOTTING HILL GROOMS

Look out for these tantalizing romances set in London's exclusive Notting Hill, written by highly acclaimed authors who, between them, have sold more than 35 million books worldwide!

Irresistible Temptation by Sara Craven
Harlequin Presents® #2077
On sale December 1999

Reform of the Playboy by Mary Lyons
Harlequin Presents® #2083
On sale January 2000

The Millionaire Affair by Sophie Weston
Harlequin Presents® #2089
On sale February 2000

Available wherever Harlequin books are sold.

HARLEQUIN®
Makes any time special ™

HARLEQUIN ⬥ PRESENTS®

Seduction SWEET REVENGE

They wanted to get even.
Instead they got...married!

by bestselling author

Penny Jordan

Don't miss Penny Jordan's latest enthralling miniseries
about four special women. Kelly, Anna, Beth and Dee
share a bond of friendship and a burning desire to
avenge a wrong. But in their quest for revenge, they
each discover an even stronger emotion.
Love.

Look out for all four books in Harlequin Presents®:

November 1999
THE MISTRESS ASSIGNMENT

December 1999
LOVER BY DECEPTION

January 2000
A TREACHEROUS SEDUCTION

February 2000
THE MARRIAGE RESOLUTION

Available at your favorite retail outlet.

HARLEQUIN®
Makes any time special ™